the whole story of half a girl

the whole story of half a girl

veera hiranandani

delacorte press

This is a work of fiction. Names, characters, places, and incidents either are the product of the author's imagination or are used fictitiously. Any resemblance to actual persons, living or dead, events, or locales is entirely coincidental.

Visit us on the Web! randomhouse.com/kids

Educators and librarians, for a variety of teaching tools, visit us at randomhouse.com/teachers

Library of Congress Cataloging-in-Publication Data
Hiranandani, Veera.
The whole story of half a girl / Veera Hiranandani. — 1st ed.
p. cm.
Summary: When Sonia's father loses his job and she must move from her small, supportive private school to a public middle school, the half-Jewish half-Indian sixth-grader experiences culture shock as she tries to navigate the school's unfamiliar social scene, and after her father is diagnosed with clinical depression, she finds herself becoming even more confused about herself and her family.
ISBN 978-0-385-74128-6 (hc) — ISBN 978-0-375-98995-7 (glb) —
ISBN 978-0-375-98441-9 (ebook)
[1. Coming of age—Fiction. 2. Racially mixed people—Fiction. 3. Depression—Fiction. 4. Middle schools—Fiction. 5. Schools—Fiction. 6. East Indian Americans—Fiction.] I. Title.
PZ7.H5977325Wh 2012
[Fic]—dc23
2011026178

The text of this book is set in 13-point Adobe Jenson Pro.

Book design by Stephanie Moss

Printed in the United States of America

10 9 8 7 6 5 4 3 2 1

First Edition

Random House Children's Books supports the First Amendment and celebrates the right to read.

For David, Hannah, and Eli—
my biggest fans

chapter one

I'm in school, sitting with my hair hanging long down the back of my chair, my arm around my best friend, Sam. We're planning our next sleepover. Sam's parents have the tent and sleeping bags; her mom even bought us cool spy pen-flashlights just for the occasion. To top it off, it's Friday and summer's only two weeks away.

Jack, my teacher, passes out recipes from the next and last country our fifth-grade class will be studying—India. I look down and see the makings of biryani, which is a special kind of rice dish. Jack always teaches us about the country's food first, then gives us the lay of the land and the history. Getting to know the food, Jack says, is the best way to really understand a country, just like sharing a meal with someone helps you get to know them. You can tell a lot from what a person eats. I agree. Jack always brings huge, delicious, sloppy sandwiches for his lunch, like meatball subs and Philly cheesesteaks, and that's sort of how he is—a big, friendly, messy man.

Jack takes everyone into the school kitchen and we're all assigned jobs. I have to measure the rice. Sam has to measure the spices. Other kids shell peas. Jack does all the chopping with the sharp knives. Before you know it, the rice is cooking and people are helping Jack sauté the onions, garlic, and spices. He tells everybody to stand back and holds the pan up, tossing all the ingredients like some super-famous chef, except Jack isn't a super-famous chef and half of it lands on the floor. The delicious smells swirl around my nose and make my stomach growl. I love biryani. Life's pretty good.

Then I get home. Mom's face is all droopy—the way it looks when she's upset. But she doesn't say much. She just stirs and stirs something in a pot on the stove. I look in and see a mess of purple mush. Eggplant skins and empty tofu packages sit on the counter. Tofu makes my eyes hurt. It makes my head hurt. It makes my throat hurt. My younger sister, Natasha, appears on the stairs with her drumsticks. She starts drumming on the railing and Mom tells her to practice in her room. I go off to get my homework over with. I have an essay to write on what it's like to live in India, but I don't need to do any research. I just have to ask my dad. He was born there.

Finally, at dinner, while I'm trying to figure out why the tofu is so purple, Mom says, "Kids—"

And Dad says, "Wait, I'll—"

And Mom says, "You should—"

And Natasha says, "Ha!" because she's five years younger than I am and doesn't know what to do with herself half the time.

And Dad says, "I have some bad news," which explains why Mom's acting strange and probably why the tofu's so purple. His face looks red and a little puffy, like he's going to cry. I've actually never seen my father cry. Two years ago my uncle died, Dad's brother, and Dad didn't cry at the funeral. Not that he wasn't sad, because he looked sadder than I've ever seen him.

"I lost my job. I was fired," he says. His eyes are wide.

Dad is, or was, head of sales for a company that publishes math and science textbooks. Sometimes he brings the books home. They're really heavy, with very thin pages, and are meant for college kids. They have crazy titles like *Fundamentals of Human Biology* and *An Introduction to Differential Geometry*. It makes me dizzy just looking at the covers, which are always filled with graphs, numbers, and outlines or silhouettes of someone's big smart head. Dad can understand them, though. He used to be a math professor at the same college where Mom teaches English literature. That's where they fell in love.

The reason he was fired, Dad explains, is because he had a bad quarter.

"What's a quarter?" I ask. He looks at me and tries to smile, but the corners of his mouth don't quite make it. He takes a deep breath and rubs his chin.

"It's a period of three months, a quarter of a year. Sales were down last quarter. Way down."

"Oh," I say.

A lot more questions zip through my head. Like why were the last three months so bad? Did he make someone really mad? Will he get another job? My heart speeds up, but I keep quiet. Natasha presses her fork into her purple tofu casserole, mashes it flat with the prongs.

"Who wants dessert?" Mom asks, even though we've all barely touched our dinner. She usually makes sure we've eaten enough of every weird thing she puts on the table, but I guess Mom doesn't really want to eat her tofu casserole any more than we do. I get up and help her clean off the table. She takes mint chocolate chip frozen yogurt out of the freezer and starts to heap it in big white bowls lined up on the counter. I take a bite of mine, and for a moment, the cool minty sweetness is all I can think about.

chapter two

Later that night, I find Dad in his study, hunched over the newspaper. The door's open and I poke my head in.

"I need to ask you about India," I say, hoping he's not too upset to talk to me.

He lowers the paper. "Why's that?"

"It's my final report for school. I have to find out what it's like to live there."

"Well, it's been a while since I lived in India," he says, and smiles.

I step into the room, holding my pad and pencil. "But what was it like?"

"Hot."

"I need more than *that*," I say, and plop myself on the chair in front of his desk.

"We slept on the roof at night because it was so hot."

"What did you sleep on?"

"Mats."

"What kind of food did you eat?"

"You know the kind of food we ate. Curries, pakoras, dal, rice, naan. All the stuff you've eaten." He puts the paper down, leans back, and closes his eyes.

"What did you do for fun?" I ask.

"Fun?" he says, and opens his eyes again. "My brother and I were troublemakers, so we'd make trouble for fun, I guess."

"Like how?"

"Oh, nothing that dramatic. We used to steal mangos from our neighbors' yard. They had many more mango trees than we did. And then we'd get caught and have to work in their kitchen for a few weeks."

"That's a big punishment for some mangos. Did your parents say anything to the neighbors?"

"I don't remember, but they probably agreed with the punishment. And I bet they were glad to have us out of the way," Dad says in his quiet, clipped way.

When Dad tells us about India, he always lowers his voice like he's letting us in on a secret. He doesn't really talk about his life there much. His parents both died the same year: my grandfather of a heart attack, my grandmother of cancer. Dad was only eleven, the same age I am now. His older brother, my uncle, died four years ago of a heart attack. He also has two younger sisters, my aunties. After their parents' deaths, they all lived with different relatives until they finally came here to America. I guess they just wanted to leave it all behind. I wonder if he misses it, though.

We went to India last year, to Bombay, where my dad was born, and to Agra, to see the Taj Mahal. Bombay is called Mumbai now, but Dad still calls it Bombay. On the way to the Taj Mahal we passed fields where dyed silk saris lay flat on the ground drying, the billowing colors bright and new against the dusty grass. Dad was like the colors of those saris when we were there. He showed us everything he could, smiling tons, chatting in Sindhi with people he knew from many years ago. I've never seen him so happy.

"Tell me more about the trouble you got into," I say to him.

Dad rubs his face with both hands. "I want to help you, I do. When's your report due?" he says, looking up, blinking.

"In a couple of days," I tell him, but it's actually due tomorrow.

"Is it all right if we talk more tomorrow, then?"

"Sure." I know I'll just end up Googling what I need for the rest. "Dad, is everything going to be okay?"

"It'll be fine," he says, leaning over to kiss my forehead. "Now get some sleep."

• • •

A week later, when Natasha and I are in the bathroom getting ready for bed, Mom knocks on the door even though it's halfway open. Natasha's sitting on the toilet and I'm brushing my teeth. Natasha always sings in the bathroom, and she's pretty bad, but I find myself brushing to the beat anyway as she belts out "When the Saints Go Marching In" at the top of her lungs.

"Girls," Mom says. She only calls us "girls" when she's mad or has bad news. Natasha stops singing. I stop brushing. "I'm afraid that next week will be your last at Community. You'll both be starting public school in September."

I look at Natasha and she starts crying. She gets up and flushes the toilet, still in tears. Mom hugs her and smooths her hair back. I don't cry. I don't believe what Mom has just said. I spit and rinse.

"I know you might feel sad now," she says, "but it'll be an exciting new experience. I promise."

Natasha and I have always gone to Community. It's different from other schools. All the classes are really small. Everyone sits around a big table instead of desks, and we call our teachers by their first names. We don't have to raise our hands for permission to speak or go to the bathroom. This doesn't mean everyone just does whatever they want. We have rules, and most of the time everybody listens. I've been in class with the same ten kids since kindergarten, and Jack's been our teacher for the last two years. I don't know how to be in another kind of school—the kind I've read about where thirty kids have to walk in line and call their teachers Mr. This and Ms. That. I stop looking at Natasha and look at Mom. She has tears in her eyes too.

"Does this have to do with Dad being fired?" I ask. Asking a lot of questions normally makes me feel better. Dad says it's good that I like to ask questions, because it will make me a better journalist, which is what I want to be someday. Since this whole thing happened, I've been afraid to ask questions. This question, though, just flies right out of me.

"Yes and no," Mom answers.

I wait for her to say more. Natasha waits too, sticking her finger in her ear and scratching it good.

"This change was inevitable, honey," Mom goes on.

"What's iniv-table?" Natasha asks. Mom always uses big words. That's her thing, being an English professor.

"It means it had to happen sooner or later. Community only goes up to eighth grade, you know that. We didn't plan on making such an abrupt change, but Dad and I have been worried that you're not getting enough at Community. Enough of the basics."

I'm not sure what she could possibly mean. I have my best friend, Sam, and the greatest teacher, who takes us camping and teaches us about the world. I know how to make sushi and take sap from a tree. I know where Saudi Arabia is. Next year we're going to learn how to write an entire play and perform it. Isn't that *enough*?

"So that's the no part," I say. "What's the yes part?"

"The yes part is . . ." Mom clears her throat as she takes her pinkie nail and drags it back and forth across her lips. It's what Mom does when she's thinking. "That Community is expensive. We already pay taxes for the public schools, and they're good schools."

"And then we can go back," Natasha says, her voice as bright as the sun. "After you guys get more money?"

Mom doesn't look off into the distance anymore, but right at Natasha, as if it's the first time she's really noticing we're both there. Her face softens. "Don't worry about money, hon. That's for me and Dad to think about, and we're fine, but I don't think you'll go back."

Of course I have more questions. What's going to happen to me and Sam? How could any other teacher be as cool as Jack? I want to ask Mom, if the public schools are so good, why did she send us to Community in the first place? But I don't ask anything else. Because I'm going to Community next year, somehow.

Mom makes sure we're dressed for bed and heads to Natasha's room to read her a book. I go to my room and sit at my big dark wooden desk. It used to be Dad's until he got a bigger one for the study. The top is covered in glass and

Dad let me have his ink blotter, his stapler, and his old leather organizer, where I keep all my pens, pencils, and markers. I even have an old-fashioned fountain pen that you fill with ink. I always feel important when I sit there, like I'm the president of my room.

Right in the middle of the desk is my summer reading list, which Jack handed out today. It looks like any ordinary printout we'd get from school. But now it's the saddest piece of paper I've ever seen. I start reading the titles from the top: *The Black Pearl, From the Mixed-up Files of Mrs. Basil E. Frankweiler, The Giver, True Believer, A Wrinkle in Time . . .*

My throat catches on *A Wrinkle in Time,* one of my favorite books. Just like that, I tear the list into tiny pieces and throw them into the air. The pieces twirl and float and finally come to rest on my beige carpet.

I climb into bed. My bed is under a big window, and if I keep the curtains open I can look up and see the whole sky. On a clear night, the blinking of all those stars against the blue-black makes me feel small in a good way. My problems could never be as big as the night sky.

chapter three

Saturday comes just like it always does, but it's not just any Saturday. It's a Sleepover-at-Sam's Saturday. Normally I'd be bouncing off the walls with excitement, but instead I feel like a pile of wet newspaper. In the afternoon, Mom drops me off at Sam's house, waves to Sam's mom, Sadie, and drives away. When I see Mom's red Honda turn out of their driveway and disappear, I have to stop myself from running after her.

Sadie slices off huge hunks of her homemade raisin challah bread, slathers them with butter, makes me and Sam two plates with cold glasses of milk, and then goes off to work in her studio in the attic.

Sadie's like a second mom to me. She's a tiny lady with short spiky red hair the same color as Sam's, and she wears long skirts and big chunky silver necklaces and bracelets that she makes herself. She sells her jewelry to stores, even really fancy ones in New York City, which then sell her stuff for like a million dollars. She gives me and my mom jewelry all the time as presents. My favorite is a little silver cat pin with emerald-green eyes that she made last year for my birthday.

Sam and I take the challah and milk to her room. It's quiet since Asher, Sam's little brother, is at a friend's house. And Sam's dad, Ben, is at the café he owns. He's there a lot. Sometimes on weekends Sam and I get to help behind the counter and do stuff like make people smoothies or fill up their water.

We sit cross-legged on Sam's pink shaggy rug eating the thick, buttery bread, and of course it's amazing. Sadie makes it every Friday for Shabbat dinner. Going to Sam's for Shabbat dinner is one of my favorite things to do. The smell of just-baked bread goes so nicely with our singing, prayers, and lighting of the candles. Mom only makes Shabbat dinner if my grandparents are visiting. We don't do a lot of what other Jewish families do. I guess that's because Mom's Jewish and Dad's not. I don't even know if we count as a real Jewish family any more than we count as an Indian one.

I focus on chewing and wait for Sam to say something. Just being in Sam's room makes me feel better, though. Everything is a different color. The bunk beds are blue. Her rug is pink. The walls are green. Her dresser is yellow, all painted by Sam and Sadie. It's like living inside a rainbow.

"I can't wait for summer," she says.

I nod and chew.

"It better stop raining or we won't be able to camp."

More nodding and chewing on my part.

"What's wrong?" she says. "You haven't said much."

Once I meet her eyes I think I'm going to cry. Then I swallow a raisin the wrong way. While I cough, she smacks me on the back.

"Sonia, what's going on?" she asks after I finally stop coughing.

"I've got to tell you something," I say, my voice scratchy. "It's not good."

"Did someone die?" she asks.

"What? No. It's just—it's just that my parents said I can't go to Community next year." Then I exhale as if I've been holding my breath for a long time.

"What? Why?" she says, her mouth full of bread.

"My dad got fired from his job."

"Really?" Sam says.

"So anyway, I don't think we can afford Community anymore. But don't worry, I'll figure something out."

"Like what?" Sam asks, and chews fast now, swallowing hard. "Because you have to. We can't go to different schools. We just *can't*."

"I know. I just haven't thought of anything yet."

"We could buy a bunch of lottery tickets," Sam says.

"Are you serious?"

"Sort of. I have thirty bucks saved up. What do you have?"

"No." I shake my head and wipe some butter off my mouth. "I can't let you do that. We're just going to waste our money."

"I got it! Duh," she says as she stands up, breadcrumbs dropping to the ground. She points to the ceiling. "Apply for financial aid!"

I'm not even sure what financial aid is, exactly. I open my mouth, but before I say anything Sam goes on.

"That's what we do, although we may not have to anymore, now that my mom makes jewelry for Angelina Jolie."

"She does?"

"Well, Angelina bought a necklace that my mom made in some store."

"Wow," I say, wondering which necklace it was.

"But if you don't have enough money, you just fill out some forms and then the government gives you the amount you need."

"That's it?" I say.

"That's it," Sam says, and then she bites her lip. "At least, I think that's it." She plops herself down and takes another bite. We both chew in silence for a few seconds.

"But what if that doesn't work?" I ask.

Sam is quiet for a moment. Then she speaks. "It has to work. My cousin had a best friend and . . ." She trails off.

"What? Tell me."

"Well, her friend moved to the next town and switched schools," she says, sitting back down. She looks at me hard. "And now they're not friends anymore."

My chest feels tight. "That wouldn't happen to us," I say quickly.

"I guess not." She picks up the stuffed pink bunny she's had since she was a baby and throws it across the room. It lands in a pile of dirty clothes by her closet.

"It's not my fault, Sam," I say.

"I know," she says, twisting one of her red curls over and over into a knot.

We try to have fun after, but now Sam's the one who acts quiet and weird. She doesn't look me in the eye. Sadie makes turkey burgers out on the grill and afterward we have s'mores, but Sam suddenly doesn't feel like camping out, even though it stops raining. So we watch *E.T.* for the millionth time and go to sleep after barely talking. We don't even use the spy pen-flashlights.

Mom picks me up late the next morning, the sun already blazing down like it's the middle of July. I hug both Sadie and Sam extra hard, but Sam's arms don't hold me as tight as mine hold her.

"Jeez, Sonia, we'll see you again," Sadie says after my bear hug.

"Did you have fun?" Mom asks after we drive quietly for a few minutes.

I nod, looking out the window.

"You seem down."

"Did you know that Sam gets financial aid to go to Community?"

"A lot of people do," Mom says in a low, calm voice.

"So why can't we?"

Mom drives slowly. I can see her turning my words over in her head. "Sam said you just fill out some forms and the government gives you money."

Mom laughs. "It's a little more complicated than that."

We turn into our driveway and come to a stop in front of the garage. For some reason Mom never parks in the garage and Dad always does.

"You really love it there, huh?" she says, taking the keys out of the ignition and turning toward me.

"It's more than just school to me. I can't leave it. What about the sixth-grade play?" I tell her. "I've been waiting forever to be in that play." The play is one of the biggest things that happens at Community because the sixth graders write it and perform it themselves.

"Let me talk to Dad," Mom says. "But don't get your hopes up."

A ripple of happiness shoots through my body. Mom is good at convincing Dad to do things. She was the one who convinced him to take us to India last year. You'd think it would have been the other way around, but for some reason

Dad didn't want to go. He said the trip would be too hard on us, that Natasha and I were too young. But Mom said it was important to visit while we were still kids so that India would feel like a part of us as we grew up. She pointed out that my Indian cousins had been going every year since they were babies, and that we had already taken a big trip to Israel and that worked out fine. When he gave in and we were finally in India, he seemed to forget that it had been her idea. He kept saying things like, "Look around, kids. This is a part of who you are." So if Mom thought I needed to stay at Community, she would make it happen.

chapter four

It's our last week at school. Sam suddenly acts like she's best friends with Siri. I didn't even think she liked Siri. I don't say anything about my talk with Mom. Partly because I want to wait and surprise Sam and partly because I don't want to tell her anything good if she's going to be like this.

On Friday we have what Community calls the Summer Ceremonies. We all dress up and each class does a short performance—usually a skit or a song with a summer theme. My class recites poems we wrote. When we finish, we hand out the different-colored roses we've been holding to all the teachers and staff. After the performances, we have a huge potluck picnic. Everyone brings the most incredible food: sesame noodles, California rolls, quesadillas, fried chicken, Greek salad, samosas (from us), veggie wraps, mini quiches, huge piles of brownies and cookies, and a cooler of ice pops in every flavor imaginable. I try to have fun. I try really hard, but everything I do feels like I'm watching myself in a dream.

The next morning, Saturday, Mom and Dad knock on my door and wake me up. The full sunlight streams through my window. It must be late. Mom sits on the edge of my bed. Dad stands, with his hands on his hips.

"You awake?" Mom says.

I nod. Dad sighs and looks at Mom.

"What?" I say.

"It's about school," Dad says.

I sit up. "Did you get financial aid?"

"I'm sorry, Sonia." Dad pauses to clear his throat. "But Community isn't going to work out next year." He starts to pace across my rug.

"What happened?" I ask, rubbing my eyes.

"We wouldn't qualify for enough financial aid," Mom says. "And we don't want to take out loans."

"Why not?" I say, my voice high and whiny.

"We know this is hard for you. But give Maplewood Middle School a chance."

"You still haven't told me why you won't take out loans." I cross my arms.

Dad crosses his arms back at me and his face changes from soft to hard.

"This isn't for you to decide, Sonia. Certain things are

your decisions, and certain things are ours. This is what's best for everyone."

I keep my arms crossed and my face in a pout. Mom puts a hand on my shoulder, but I shrug it away.

"This could be good, you know. Change teaches you things," Mom says.

"The only thing this teaches me is that money makes everything better. Dad lost his job and I lost Community and probably my best friend in the whole world!"

"Sonia," Mom says, and looks at Dad.

Dad glares at me in a way I've never been glared at before. It's like he's not himself anymore. "Apparently, I've taught you nothing!" he yells. "You're just another American spoiled brat!"

Mom and I both jump. He turns and slams his hand on the side of my bookcase, which is a little wobbly. A few books thud to the floor as he stomps off. My heart is thump, thump, thumping.

Mom's always the one getting angry—because Natasha and I didn't clean our rooms or because someone left the milk out. But it's not scary angry—mean angry. Dad hardly ever loses his temper, except for now.

"Your father's upset," Mom says.

"I can see that," I say. My face melts and the tears roll, soaking Mom's sweater as she holds me on my bed. Neither of us says anything. We just hug. Then after a minute she wipes my tears with the back of her hand.

"You were a bit hard on him," she says.

I hang my head. If only I'd kept my mouth shut. I nod and start crying again.

"But he was much harder on you. He's going through a difficult time. He didn't mean it. Let's go to the pond today, okay?" she says, stroking my hair. "We'll give Dad some space. And I promise you, Sam's not going anywhere. She adores you."

I just keep quiet.

I manage to avoid Dad all day. He makes it pretty easy since he spends most of it shut in his office. Mom takes us to the pond in the next town. It's like a pool, except with no chlorine, which Mom hates the smell of, and it's a lot more muddy. I don't mind. I like the pond because it has a sandy beach and it reminds me of the ocean. There's nothing I love more than the ocean. We go to the same place on Cape Cod every August with Sam's family. The inn's right on the beach. Ben brings his guitar and we bake clams outside. Last summer on a rainy day, Sam and I sat in our pajamas on the porch of the inn and counted waves all morning. We counted 672 waves before we stopped. I wish I could be back there right now.

Even though it's only June, it's already hot and sticky. The pond water is still cold, though, and Natasha and I only manage to wade in up to our knees. We eat the almond butter–marmalade sandwiches Mom brought. Then we come home, watch TV, and eat a quick dinner, and afterward Mom disappears to do her own work, which she's been doing more and more often. My bedtime comes and goes but nobody notices. Natasha and I hang out in the den, watching more TV than we normally do. It's strangely quiet, almost as if our parents have forgotten about us. I tell Natasha she should get ready for bed. She frowns at me, but goes off to her room. I pad down the stairs. I pass Dad's study, but it's dark. I come to my parents' bedroom; the door is open a crack. There's a bit of light coming from Mom's office, which is actually the dressing area between their bedroom and bathroom.

I catch Mom's voice. I hear the words "totally unacceptable behavior."

"Don't talk to me like I'm one of the kids," Dad says.

"Then don't act like it," Mom says. "You should have seen Sonia's face after you stormed off. Next time you behave that way in front of them I swear I'll . . ." Then she stops.

I stand against the wall right outside the door. Dad coughs. Mom sniffs. I wonder if she's crying.

"You swear what?" Dad says.

Mom sniffles more. Now she's definitely crying.

"I'm sorry," Dad says. "I don't know how many times I have to say it. I wish I were perfect, but you know I'm far from that."

"I'm not the one you need to apologize to," Mom says in a low, dry voice.

Then I hear the floorboards creaking and run out of the

hallway before anyone finds me there listening. I fly upstairs and dive into bed and start reading the paper. Mom always saves me the travel section of the *New York Times*. I love imagining myself in all those strange, beautiful places. I cut out the articles from the places I plan to go to someday—Africa, Alaska, Italy, Greece. I want to go back to India. I like the way there are flowers everywhere: climbing walls, bunched in hotels, floating in fountains. I like the way everyone sits on the floor at parties, and how all the women drape themselves in beautiful silk saris and gold jewelry just to go to the market. I like the warm smell of spices and fruit everywhere. I like that when I look around I see so many people who look like Dad, even like me.

I hear Dad's heavy steps coming up the stairs. I read the title of the article "The Magic of Madrid" over and over.

"Hi," he says, poking his head into my open door.

"Hi," I say back and keep staring at the paper.

"It's hard for me, sometimes," he says.

I nod.

"I grew up with very little. You have so much. Mom and I have wanted you and Natasha to have lots of opportunities, and we've worked hard to give them to you. But I also wish I could give you . . ." He stops and rubs his forehead. "I hoped I *had* given you some perspective. I would have been so lucky to go to a school like Maplewood, let alone Community. In my school we sat on the floor, held slates on our laps, and tried not to get bitten by scorpions."

I keep staring at the paper. Dad watches me, then puts a hand on my back. I squirm a little and he takes it away.

"Sonia, say something," he says gently.

"Do you ever want to go back?"

"Go back where?"

"To India."

"No," he says, all serious and low, looking straight at me. "We're better off here. Trust me."

"Dad, is it okay if I miss Community?" My voice breaks a little bit. I don't want to cry. "I've gone there for so long. All my friends are there."

"Of course it is, but how do I get you to understand how lucky you are?"

"I understand," I say.

His face relaxes. "Okay," he says, standing up. "Good night, then." He kisses me on the forehead and leaves.

None of this would have happened if I hadn't gotten all whiny about Community, or let Mom see how upset I was when Dad got mad at me. Before, in their room, they sounded like they hated each other, like they wanted to spit their words at the other person. If only I could have just acted normal about the whole thing.

I sit cross-legged on my bed and look around my room. I

look at the big, heavy furniture, the soft rug, my blue and green tie-dyed comforter and matching pillows, my closet full of clothes and toys, my bookshelf full of books. I think of my dad in India sleeping on a mat on a roof covered with mosquito nets. I think of him sweating in his dusty schoolroom with his little chalkboard. I think of him stealing a mango for fun. Here I am, the luckiest girl in the world, but all I can think of is what I don't have.

chapter five

"Sonia, up, up," Dad says, waking me on the first day of school, my new school. He's been home all summer while Mom's been teaching a lot more classes. At first I thought he'd be moping about his job, but it's been exactly the opposite. Some days we just want to lie around and watch TV, but Dad won't let us. He also does most of the cooking now—whipping up things like hot pepper omelets and strawberry waffles. He grills a lot too, turkey dogs and burgers. Or he makes a curry or naan pizza. I never knew this, but Dad's a much better cook than Mom. And there's not a block of tofu in sight.

Mom and Dad seem comfortable with each other now, not like they were when Dad first lost his job. I keep spying on them just to make sure. So far I haven't heard any more arguments. Once in a while Dad will be quiet at dinner or get really annoyed with something small, like the way the kitchen faucet always drips no matter how many times he fixes it, or the neighbors' barking dog. He'll start stomping around, muttering things under his breath, swearing and speaking in Sindhi. But Mom just asks him in a way that's not really a question if he wants some time to himself. He usually marches off to his study. When we see him again he doesn't seem upset anymore.

I wonder what he does in his study that makes him feel better. Maybe he just imagines himself in magical, exciting places like I do. Maybe he thinks of India, not the hard and miserable part, but the running around with his brother, hands sticky from stolen mangos.

Along with making lots of food, he's been taking me and Natasha to the big park for hikes or swims at the pond. Then we go play tennis at the town courts if it isn't raining. We've been to the make-your-own-pottery store three times and gone to four puppet shows, seven sing-alongs, and ten story-times. The storytimes are too young for me, but Dad seems to like them so much I don't want to disappoint him. We've also been helping him with projects around the house: We all painted the laundry room. We cleaned out the garage. We planted new hydrangeas in the garden. We even started building a tree house.

I've never seen him like this, always coming up with a new activity, always in motion, always here with us. Anytime

I want to relax, I go to my room because I know that if he sees me, he'll rope me into another project. When he asks, there's something in his eyes now that makes me afraid to say no.

I've been hanging out with Sam nearly every weekend too, mostly at her house. She wasn't happy that I wouldn't be back at Community, but after we hadn't talked for a week, she called one morning at seven o'clock. I was still asleep. Dad came in with the cordless.

"It's not going to happen to us," her voice chirped on the other end. "I know I've been a jerk. I'm sorry."

I coughed a little, blinked my eyes, and wondered if I was dreaming. But I wasn't.

"Good," I said.

Mom let Sam sleep over that night. Sam brought the spy pen-flashlights. Mom let us put the pop-up tent in my room and we had a pretend campout. We talked and talked and talked until midnight.

For the rest of the summer, at Sam's house, we'd bead bracelets or spin on the tire swing that hangs from the big oak tree in her backyard. We didn't go to Cape Cod, and I'm pretty sure it was because it was too expensive, but Dad said it was because our favorite inn was already filled. Sam's family decided to visit her aunt in Maine instead. We don't talk about that, though, and we don't talk about the fact that we're going to different schools soon. Instead we ask her Magic 8

Ball stuff like when we'll have our first kiss from a boy, and if I'll be a journalist and if Sam will be an actress, and what countries we'll travel to as a famous journalist and actress, and if Sam will ever get to meet Zac Efron.

I kept hoping, on those lazy days under the big oak tree, that somehow summer would just keep going and I'd never get here—where I am this morning. About to get up, get dressed, and go to Maplewood Middle School.

"Sonia," Dad says. "Up, up, you have a big day ahead of you."

I pull the covers tight around my face. "Just a few more minutes."

"Come on, you're starting an adventure." Dad pats my stomach through the covers. That's what he calls everything these days, an adventure. I'm tired of adventures. I pull the blanket down so just my eyes show. Even though I've spent a lot of time with him lately, I feel like we haven't really talked.

"Dad? What will it be like, my new school?" I ask.

"You'll make new friends, learn different things. In a week it'll be like you never went anywhere else."

"Are you going to get a new job?" I ask and as I'm saying it, I realize it's the one question I've wanted to ask him all summer.

He's quiet for a few seconds and doesn't look at me, just straightens the covers.

"I'm enjoying my time off, enjoying spending time with

you kids," he says, still looking down. Then he meets my eyes. "But yes, soon I'll get a new job. Better get up, though. It's getting late." He puts his warm hand on my cheek before standing up and leaving my room.

I get dressed and go down to breakfast with my stomach doing cartwheels. I have to wait for the bus. Natasha does too, but she goes in later and she's still young enough that Dad will wait with her. I wish he'd wait with me, but the other kids at the bus stop would probably laugh. I've never taken a bus to school before. Mom either drove us or we'd carpool. But this morning she hands me my lunch, gives me a hard hug, and leaves to teach her class. I hear her red Honda pull out of the garage and rumble down the long gravel driveway.

I'm surprised that all Dad made on such a big morning is oatmeal, but it's just as well. I can barely get down half a bowl. Dad and Natasha follow me to the door as I set off for the bus stop. Natasha waves frantically. I don't turn around after that, but I know Dad is there watching. I can still feel his warm hand on my cheek, could draw an outline of it resting there.

The driveway ends and I head onto Willow Lane. Usually I love that our house is set way back in the woods, so that we can only see trees and grass. But today all those trees are blocking my view of everything that lies before me—and I'm getting nervous.

After I round the corner, I finally see two girls and a very tall boy standing across the street. I've seen them before, blankly waiting for the bus as we zipped by in Mom's warm car on the way to Community. I suck in my breath and walk slower. The first thing I notice is that they aren't carrying lunch bags. The banana, carrot juice, and tuna fish sandwich I'm holding suddenly feel pounds heavier as they slosh around in my brown paper bag. Before I cross the street, I roll up the bag and shove it into my knapsack. The two girls are talking all hush-hush with each other. The boy stands a few feet away and has earphones stuck in his ears. He wears a black baseball cap and bops his head to the music. I walk toward a big rock about ten feet away from them and start to sit down.

"I wouldn't sit there," says one of the girls as she gives her honey-blond hair a toss. Her eyes flicker at me for a moment and she twists her white sneaker into the blacktop. The other girl, who has a chubby face and dark hair, looks me up and down.

"Why?" I ask.

The chubbier girl says, "Bird poop."

"Oh," I say. I quickly stand up and turn around to look at the rock. It shimmers its clean gray and silver surface back at me.

The blond girl asks, "Did you just move here?"

"No. I used to go to another school, The Community School."

"Never heard of it," the chubby girl says.

"It's in Weston," I say, which is the next town over. She just shrugs. The boy looks me over for a second and goes back to his head-bopping.

"What are your names?" I ask.

"Cindy," the chubby girl says, and looks at her friend.

"Heather," the other girl answers.

"I'm Sonia," I tell them both.

"What's your last name?" Cindy asks.

"Nadhamuni."

"Say what?" Heather says.

Every time I say my last name for the first time, people always ask me to say it again or spell it three times, and they still can never get it right. The funny thing is that it sounds exactly the way it's spelled: *Nad-ha-muni*, and I really have no idea why it's harder to pronounce than any other long last name. At Community everyone knew how to say it. I repeat it for them. They both squint.

"Where are you from?" Cindy asks.

"Here," I say.

"But your name. Where's that from?"

"My father's from India," I say.

"Oh, like does he wear feathers in his hair and stuff?" Cindy still squints. Heather giggles softly behind her.

"Why would he wear feathers in his hair?" I ask.

"He's not that kind of Indian, idiot," Heather says to

Cindy and nudges her in the arm. Cindy shrugs. "He probably wears a turban, right?" Heather crosses her arms, pleased with herself.

"Uh, no." I start to explain, but thankfully we hear the gears of the yellow bus lumbering up the hill. Everyone turns to watch. It comes to a cranky, squeaky stop and we all climb on. Cindy and Heather head toward the back with the tall boy. I sit in the first empty seat I see in the front. I can't believe I'll have to wait at the bus stop with Cindy and Heather every day.

chapter six

When we arrive in front of Maplewood Middle School, I see at least a hundred kids, some still on the buses lined up along the sidewalk, some gathered in clusters on the school stairs, others playing with hacky sacks or skateboards.

I push my way past the groups and walk in, my heart racing, the saliva gone from my tongue. I'm supposed to go to the main office first, so someone can escort me to my classroom, but I don't see it. I visited the school a week before with Mom, and I thought it was to my right. But now I only see two closed brown doors, no open area with a woman sitting at the front desk. I clutch the registration slip that lists my schedule.

A bell rings and tons of kids come barreling through the front glass doors. I stand still, hoping not to be trampled. A girl runs into me, knocks my backpack clean off my shoulder, and doesn't say she's sorry. The top isn't zipped all the way and out tumble my notebook and lunch. Before I can bend down to pick them up, another kid steps on my lunch bag as he runs. In a flash everybody is gone, tucked away in classrooms. I gather up my stuff, walk around the corner, and continue down a long hallway. All I can hear are the echoing voices of people inside classrooms like ghosts in the walls.

I walk faster and faster and feel a little dizzy. I make a left, then another right, and walk down a few more hallways, knowing that I've lost my starting point. I start to run, though I'm not sure if I'm running toward something or away from it, and just as I round another corner I run smack into a grown-up.

"And where are you supposed to be?" a tall man in a gray sweat suit asks me. He has a basketball under his arm and sparkly blue eyes.

I try to speak, but my throat catches on a bump of air. I swallow and start again. "I, where's the . . . ?" is all I can manage, so I just thrust the registration slip at him.

He takes the paper, looks at it, and frowns. "Oh, I'm afraid you've got the wrong school."

"But my mom—" Before I can finish, or cry, or do anything else, he puts a heavy, warm hand on my shoulder.

"I'm just kidding. Your homeroom's actually right over there, Mrs. Langley's," he says, grinning, and points to a yellow door a little ways down the hallway. I'd like to be mad at him, but his smile nearly jumps off his face.

"Really?"

"You're in the right place"—he looks at my paper for a second—"Miss Nadhamuni." My heart lights up. He says it perfectly. "I'm Mr. Totono, your friendly neighborhood gym teacher." I follow him to Mrs. Langley's classroom and he opens the door. If more people are like this guy here, I think, it might not be so bad.

"Mrs. Langley," Mr. Totono says, "may I present Miss Sonia Nadhamuni."

Mrs. Langley is standing to the side of her desk. She's only inches taller than I am, with short salt-and-pepper hair and a nose that looks like a pig's. She clasps her hands in front of her brown dress and grimaces.

"Welcome, Sonia. Please find a seat," she says, and gestures toward the rows of desks and checks me off on her attendance sheet. The kids, folded solemnly in their desk chairs, stare at me. All twenty-five of them. No circular tables here. No Sam. No Jack.

I find one of only two empty desks in the third row near the windows and try to settle in. Someone has written stuff on my desktop in blue pen. It says two things: *MF+DG* and *GB smells.*

Mrs. Langley makes some general announcements and then the next bell rings. Since Mrs. Langley is also my English teacher for next period, I stay. Some kids leave and new ones file in. When the bell rings again, Mrs. Langley starts to talk about words, the importance of words, how they give us power, grace, the ability to connect with other people. It actually sounds kind of exciting, until she tells the class she's going to give vocabulary quizzes every week. I've never taken a quiz. At Community we had some spelling and math tests, but mostly we just wrote essays or stories or created projects.

I feel relieved when Mrs. Langley says we won't have our new textbooks until next week. But then she takes out a huge stack of vocabulary lists and holds them in her upright palm like a pizza.

"Hi," whispers a girl in the desk next to mine as Mrs. Langley starts making her rounds with the lists. The sun flashes on her shiny blond French braid, making it look like gold. I smile at her and she sends a folded piece of bright pink polka-dotted stationery onto my desk. She gives me a quick nod as Mrs. Langley starts down my aisle. I grab the note and stuff it in my pocket when she's turned the other way. The starchy feel of the thick paper stays on my fingers. Mrs. Langley moves toward me. She lingers between me and the girl with the braid and gives us our lists. I hold my breath. I'm actually going to get in trouble on the first day of school.

The girl looks up at Mrs. Langley and flashes her a white, toothy smile. Mrs. Langley finally moves past us with a *swish, clomp, swish, clomp* of her rough dress and heavy shoes. I can't tell if she saw the note and has decided to ignore it or didn't see it at all. When she's on the other side of the room, I fish it out and open it.

> I think your purple jeans are really cool.
> Want to sit together at lunch?
>
> Kate

Kate signs the note with a heart at the end. I corner-eye her blond braid, pink shirt, and designer jeans suspiciously while she reads her vocabulary list. Nobody at Community looks quite like Kate. Take Sam, for instance. Sam has frizzy red hair and green eyes and she loves rainbows. She has rainbow T-shirts, rainbow barrettes, rainbow belts. Everyone at Community has their own style. I like to wear my wavy black hair as long as possible. I love purple too. I have purple jeans, lots of purple shirts, and even purple sneakers. Everyone here seems to dress alike. They all wear some version of a button-down in pink or white or blue with jeans or khakis. Some of the girls wear tank tops underneath. I stick out like a wart in my purple jeans and my lucky yellow T-shirt that has a picture of the Eiffel Tower on it. But at least Kate likes my jeans.

I stuff the note back in my pocket and check out my vocabulary list. The first word is "*Nebulous* (adj): unclear and lacking form. Synonym: cloudy." Just the word I've been looking for.

"How was it?" Mom asks that night at dinner.

Natasha pops a radish from the salad into her mouth and crunches down. "We sang a lot," she answers first.

"Sang?" Mom asks.

"Yeah, three songs. And there was a kid, Barry, who pinched me on the playground, but then this other girl, Sarah, said he always pinches everyone, and then we went on the swings."

"So it was a good day?" Mom asks her. I'm surprised Mom didn't grill Natasha about the pinching thing. Normally that's something she'd be all worried about. But Mom's jumpy tonight. She's gotten up four times to get more napkins or another pitcher of water or to refill the bowl of broccoli.

"Pretty good. Mrs. Price is funny."

I can tell that in a week it will be like *she* never went to any other school. If Natasha likes a new thing, she just packs her bags and follows it without looking back. All I can think of is calling Sam after dinner.

"And Sonia, how'd it go for you?" Mom asks, turning her nervous face to me. Then she glances at Dad, who's staring at his empty plate, rubbing his chin, a million miles away. He stops rubbing and smiles a sheepish smile.

"It was okay."

"Just okay?" Mom says.

"Yeah. I kind of got lost in the morning."

"How lost?" Dad asks.

"I couldn't find my homeroom and then the gym teacher helped me."

"Doesn't sound too bad. How are your teachers?" he asks.

"Okay, I guess. My English teacher said she's going to give us lots of vocabulary tests." And her dress was ugly and she sort of looks like a pig, I want to say. And my day wasn't okay; it made me feel like an alien from Mars.

I lost sight of Kate as we herded into the cafeteria like sheep. By the time I spotted her again, she was already surrounded by a bunch of girls in my class, all talking and laughing. She looked up and noticed me but didn't say anything, not a wave, not a smile. I certainly wasn't going to plop myself down in the middle of all her matching-shirt friends.

Then I saw a table to the left where a girl was sitting

alone, writing in a notebook. She was in my English class too. Something made me want to ask her what she was writing. Suddenly I didn't care about Kate or anyone else, so I tugged up my jeans and went over to her.

"Can I sit here?" I asked.

She looked up from her notebook, gave me the once-over, and nodded.

"Hey, is that the Eiffel Tower?" she asked.

"Yeah," I said, sitting down across from her.

"Did you go there?"

"Last spring with my parents."

"Wow! Was it the most romantic place in the world?"

She put her elbows on the table, rested her chin on her hands, and closed her eyes for a few seconds. I wasn't sure if Paris was romantic, but it had lots of parks and cool old buildings and a river that ran through the entire city. And once, at night after dinner, when we were walking by the river, the Eiffel Tower suddenly lit up and sparkled like a million stars. That was my favorite part of Paris. Come to think of it, though, Mom and Dad did a lot of hand-holding in Paris, which they never do at home, so maybe it was romantic.

"It was really pretty," I said.

"When I get older, I'm going to live there and be a writer," she said, and patted her notebook as she closed it. Her name was written in big black letters on the front: *Alisha Brooks*.

"I want to be a writer too—a journalist—and travel all over the world," I told her. My body relaxed. Even my smashed sandwich started tasting better. I was about to ask her what she wrote about, but a group of kids descended on our table. In seconds everything became a swirling blur of orange lunch trays, laughter, and metal chairs scraping the floor.

Nobody seemed to mind that I was sitting at the table. Actually, nobody seemed to notice me. But I noticed me. I was used to being darker-skinned than everyone at Community except for Marshal, whose parents are from Trinidad, but everyone at this table made me stick out like a ghost. The kids who sat here were black, while all the other tables were filled with white kids. Alisha told some of the other kids that I had been to Paris. They seemed less impressed but asked me some questions, mostly about the Eiffel Tower. I answered, ate my sandwich, and tried not to think of Community. Or why the white kids and black kids didn't sit together here. Or where you were supposed to sit if you were too dark to be white and too light to be black? And that was how my day went.

"Well, don't worry," Mom says. "These things take time. It'll get easier."

"Dad?" I ask. "Would you call yourself black or white?"

Dad puts down his fork and coughs a little. Mom freezes in mid-bite. Natasha even looks up from mashing her broccoli to bits.

"Why? Did something happen at school?" Dad says, and moves around in his chair a little.

"Nope. Just wondering."

"Neither," he says. "I'm Indian."

"But if you had to pick one," I say.

"White, I guess."

"But you're not white," I say.

"I'm not black either. Indian is considered Caucasian, which is technically white. Or at least it was when I was growing up."

Mom steps in. "Sonia, do you want to know what you should call yourself?"

"I guess white, right?"

"It's up to you how you want to identify yourself. You could call yourself white, or half Indian. Or even half South Asian American."

"Yeah, but there's the Jewish part too."

"But that's your religion, not your ethnicity."

"Sometimes people who are half white and half black call themselves black because they look black," I say. "So I could call myself Indian and not white at all, since I look Indian. But according to Dad Indian is white. Only it's not white. Dad's skin looks a lot closer to black than white."

Dad looks at his hands and turns them faceup and facedown as if it's the first time he's ever seen them.

"How do you see yourself?" he asks.

"I don't know. I thought you guys were supposed to tell me."

Mom and Dad look at each other.

"Are you sure nothing happened at school to bring this all up?" Mom asks.

"Yup. Just curious. No big deal." If I tell them about the way the white kids and black kids don't sit together at lunch, Mom would race to call the PTA and arrange some kind of multicultural day. She did that stuff at Community, but Community was already blended together.

Mom lets a breath out and seems relieved to be done with the conversation. Dad's lost in his thoughts. I ask to be excused and run up to the den to dial the white push-button phone. Sam answers and her voice spreads over me like a mouthful of chocolate.

"Hi, it's me."

"Hi," Sam says, sounding less excited than I had hoped. "How was it?"

"Well, I survived. The place is huge," I say, and swallow hard. Before I called, I couldn't wait to tell Sam about Kate and Alisha and the strange way everyone sat in the cafeteria. Now the words seem too heavy to hold on my tongue. "But I want to know more about your day. Tell me everything," I say instead, knowing it will hurt. Sometimes that kind of pain feels good, like a scab you just have to pick at even though you know you shouldn't. She tells me they made fortune cookies and Jack had everyone do trust falls at recess. And he said there was going to be more math this year. And everybody has to think of a project for the science fair in October. *And* they're already starting to write the play for November. I pretend I don't hear that part.

"And," she says, "Siri wears a bra now."

"Whoa!" The word "bra" rings in my ears. I look down at my board of a chest. Siri wears a bra now. "Does she really need one?" I ask, laughing.

"I think so," Sam says. "What's so funny about it?"

"I don't know. It's just that last year we were . . ." I stop. I don't know what I want to say anymore.

"I'd better go. My mom's calling me," Sam says.

"Okay." After we hang up, I lie down on the rug and stay there for a while, alone in the den, holding the phone in my hand.

chapter eight

The next day at school I see Alisha get off her bus. It's a different bus, blue and white instead of yellow. I recognize some of the kids from lunch who get off with her. Alisha looks up at me and I wave. She waves back and starts walking toward me. Her hair is scraped back in a tight bun like it was yesterday. She looks older than the rest of the kids here—taller, at least.

"Hi," she says, and clutches her notebook to her chest.

"Hi," I say back. And we walk through the front doors together. "Why isn't your bus yellow?" I ask her.

"It's a city bus from Bridgeport, where I live," she says, searching my face, expecting something from me. What, I don't know.

"Cool" is the only word I can think of. I thought everybody who went to this school had to live in my town. Bridgeport was pretty far away.

"Some kids in my neighborhood are bussed here because our school isn't that good," she explains, and looks at me hard and straight. She's really good at eye contact. My mother always tells me to make eye contact with people, but I don't like anyone's eyes on me too long these days.

"Oh, right," I say, like I know all about it. Why only some kids? Why do some people have to go to the bad school and what's wrong with it anyway? I want to ask these things, but I don't.

"Did you just move here?" she asks.

"No. I went to a different school," I say. She asks where and has an excited edge to her voice. It feels so good to tell someone who I am and where I came from. I tell her about Jack and Sam. I tell her about the food Jack taught us how to make. I tell her about the stories and plays we wrote, and the sixth-grade play that I'll miss, and all the camping trips I've gone on. I feel like I'm describing a foreign land and she drinks it in, doesn't say a word until I'm done.

"That's not real. It can't be real," she says, rushed and sputtering. "I wish I could go to that school. How come you don't anymore?"

"Well, my dad lost his job and we can't afford it." After these words fall out of my mouth, my chest tightens. Maybe I'm not supposed to tell people this.

"Oh, it's a *private* school," she says as she stops walking. "Did you have to wear uniforms? My cousin goes to boarding school and he wears one. He has tons of homework and the teachers are really strict and lots of the kids are really snobby and rich. All everybody talks about is getting into Harvard."

"Community isn't like that," I say. Before I can say anything else, the bell rings and we rush to our separate homerooms.

Later that morning during English, another pink polka-dotted note comes flying onto my desk.

> Hi! Sorry we didn't sit together at lunch yesterday. Do you want to today? Check out Mrs. Langley's shoes. Could they be any more grandma?
>
> Kate

I wanted to sit with Alisha, but maybe Alisha doesn't believe me and thinks I went to one of those fancy private schools like her cousin goes to. Maybe she thinks I'm rich and snobby. Maybe I am, I don't even know anymore.

What's funny is that at Maplewood, the school that people don't need extra money to go to, everyone seems to have plenty of money. The kids show off their iPods and cell phones, something my parents would never buy me. We don't even have cable TV. I see other parents dropping off their kids in fancy cars like Mercedes and BMWs.

At Community nobody seemed to care so much about what they wore, and no one had iPods. But Alisha isn't like most kids here. She's wearing the same black T-shirt and jeans she had on yesterday. And she doesn't seem to have an iPod or a cell phone either. But if she doesn't like me just because I went to private school, that's not really fair.

Mrs. Langley paces across the front of the room in a gray dress and rubbery gray shoes. *Swish, clomp, swish, clomp*. She writes more vocabulary words on the board, the chalk crumbling in her hand—*"efficient," "formulate," "genre," "hazardous"* . . . I wonder if that's all we're going to learn?

I write my reply under a cupped hand and throw it onto Kate's desk.

But how do I know you mean it?

Sonia

Kate's eyebrows knit together as she reads it. I wonder if she can make out my handwriting. Most of the time I think much faster than I can write and it comes out like "chicken scratch," as Mom calls it. Each letter in Kate's handwriting looks like a fat little happy man. It's chunky and neat, every letter the same height. She writes something back and looks around. My heart beats faster and I can feel sweat tingling under my arms. Maybe I need deodorant. The note lands on my desk.

> I'll meet you by your locker just before lunch.
>
> xxoo,
> Kate

I look over at her and smile. Her head is bent over a lavender piece of paper as she writes another note. I wonder if she writes notes to people all day. A few minutes later she chucks it at another girl, one of the three Jessicas in our class. This Jessica is short and wears her long brown hair in a high ponytail. She also wears really tight clothes. She's always chewing on her nails, giving people sideways looks, and whispering in Kate's ear.

Just before lunch I walk slowly to my locker, wondering if Kate will be there. She isn't. I open it and grab my lunch, another tuna sandwich, but this time with green apples chopped up the way I like. Mom even put in a piece of nut candy from my aunty, who brings a ton back every time she visits India. It's made from cashew nuts and has the thinnest shaving of real silver on top. When I eat it, I feel like the Indian children's book princess my parents named me after.

"Hi," I hear behind my back. I whip around. Kate stands there, her hands on her hips, blue eyes shining.

"Ready?" she says.

"Yup." I close my locker and clutch the paper bag. Her hands are empty. I wonder if she doesn't eat lunch and then I remember that the cafeteria sells food. Yesterday tons of kids lined up for chicken nuggets, hamburgers, and hot dogs. My old school didn't have a cafeteria.

"Oh, you brought," she says, eyeing my lunch bag.

"Uh-huh," I say, like I'm carrying a bag of dead rats. Jessica comes up to both of us and we join the flow of the crowd shuffling toward the cafeteria as all the kids pour out of their classrooms. Out of the corner of my eye I see Alisha meet up with some of the other kids from Bridgeport.

"So I heard Peter Hanson likes you," Jessica says to Kate. Then she flashes her eyes over me, doesn't say a word, and turns back to Kate as she twirls her thick ponytail. Her fingernails are painted bright red. Mom would never let me wear red nail polish, even though my ten-year-old cousin has worn nail polish since she was like four years old. But Mom says nice Jewish girls don't.

"Shhhh," Kate hisses, "he might hear you." Then she bends toward me.

"That's Peter. Right. Over. There."

I glance over my shoulder in the direction of where she's pointing. She grabs my arm.

"Don't look!" Jessica whispers fiercely. I'm not sure why everything has to be so top secret. And it's not that I don't like boys. I do. I've even been in love before.

Connor O'Reilly was one out of four boys in my old class. The other boys were just my friends and so was Connor, until one day out of the clear blue sky I noticed how long his eyelashes were. Last fall, our whole class took a hike to an old cemetery to do grave rubbings. Connor and I had stopped in front of the same gravestone. At first I noticed the stone because there was a big dove imprinted on the front that was perfect for a rubbing. Then we looked closer. It said:

Grace Wheeler
Our precious little bird. Too short a flight.
May God keep you in peace.
1914–1919

I sucked in my breath when I read the dates and everything around me went slow and heavy. The other kids stepped around the crushed leaves and sticks with their rolls of paper and charcoal. Grace Wheeler's whole life had only been five years long. Connor knelt beside me and traced the dove in the stone with his finger. I looked at him and his eyes were down. They were the most beautiful eyelashes I'd ever seen. Suddenly I felt shivery and warm and wanted to hold his hand. It made me feel okay about Grace Wheeler, because Connor and I were there together, sitting with her. After that, Connor wasn't just Connor anymore. But Sam liked him too, and since there were six girls and only four boys in our class, everyone had to share. I was sure I loved Connor more than Sam did, but Connor said he liked us both the same.

We make it to the cafeteria and the noise is deafening. Teachers are calling out things like "Slow down, everybody" and "Shhhhh" and "No running!" Jessica and Kate go over to the line at the lunch counter. I don't know what to do. It's stupid to stand in line if I'm not getting any food, but I don't want to go and sit at the table without Kate.

"Hey, stand in line with us," she says, and pulls me toward her and Jessica. She's a little grabby, but in a good way, like she's stopping me from falling.

"Who told you about Peter?" Kate asks Jessica. She seems calm now, like she doesn't care. Jessica's eyes light up.

"Ann told me. She heard it from Liz."

I reach the lady at the big metal counter and back away to let Kate and Jessica order. The lady is very fat, with cheeks as red as tomatoes. She has her hair bunched inside a net and looks really angry. Kate and Jessica order the same thing—chicken nuggets and M&M's. Mom would flip if I ate like this. The only junk food we ever have in the house is ice cream or oatmeal cookies. The fat lady turns around and grabs packs of candy off a shelf, and little cardboard containers of the chicken nuggets from under an orange heat lamp.

I walk behind Kate and Jessica as they march over to the same table they sat at yesterday. It's all girls. At Alisha's table the boys and girls sit together. I sit on one side of Kate and Jessica sits on the other. Most people have cafeteria food, but one girl starts unwrapping what looks like a bologna sandwich. I can tell from the pink Band-Aid color, the round edges of meat. A bag of corn chips sits by her too. Another girl has potato chips and cookies and some kind of sandwich, possibly turkey, on white bread. The rest have chicken nuggets.

A group of boys in our grade sit at the table right behind us. One of them, Peter Hanson, throws a paper airplane over at us. It floats above my head and lands right on top of my tuna sandwich.

"Open it," Kate says, her voice hushed and excited.

My fingers feel shaky as I unfold the airplane because everyone at the table is staring. *Hi, Kate,* it says. I read it out loud. It all seems so funny—the airplane note, the little pieces of chicken nuggets, the round bologna meat, the boys at one table and the girls at the other. I roll my eyes. Kate starts to laugh. Then I start and I can't stop. My laughter spills over to Kate and she grabs me again, holds on to my arm, and we both tumble around in our sounds for a few more seconds before we stop, wiping laugh tears from our eyes. Jessica just stares at us.

"What's so funny?" she asks over a mouthful of M&M's.

"Nothing," Kate says, and grins. A leftover giggle ripples through me. The cafeteria must be a hundred degrees.

Kate crumples up the airplane and tosses it behind her. I don't dare turn around to see where it lands. Then I catch Alisha looking at me all the way from her table, but she turns away. She unpacks her lunch and takes out her notebook. She bends over it, pen in hand.

chapter nine

When I get home from school, Dad's study door is closed and Mom's not home. I open the fridge and take out a small carton of hummus and a bunch of baby carrots. Natasha's already watching TV in the den because she gets home a half hour earlier than I do.

"Mom said only an hour a day," I warn as I flop down next to her on the couch.

"I know," she says, making a face. "I have a half hour more." She holds out her hand for some carrots.

"Get your own," I say, shoving her hand away. I look back at the TV. Tom's building a mousetrap for Jerry out of matchsticks. Then Tom catches Jerry in the mousetrap and strikes a match, but Jerry chews his way out the back of the trap before it bursts into flames and catches Tom's tail on fire. I sit back, certain of what's coming next. I feel the rush of energy from her before it happens. Natasha turns and tackles me. The carrots and hummus go flying. Even though she's smaller than me, she's strong, a "little powerhouse," as Mom says. I grab her arm and twist it.

"Ow! Cut it out!" she yells.

"You made me drop everything!" I yell back, and twist her arm more before letting go. She grabs my hair. "Get off," I say, and grab her arms again. We fight a lot lately and for some reason it feels good. I'm not even that angry with her. I wonder if she likes it too. We both keep on yelling, shoving, and grabbing. My hand goes into the hummus. I'm about to wipe some on her face when I hear Dad.

"Girls!" Our father appears at the door like a big, dark shadow. He's still in his bathrobe. His face looks gray as stone. We freeze for a moment to take him in, and then yell over each other, trying to explain the fight, blaming each other for different things.

"I don't care what happened!" Dad yells so loud I feel sick. "Clean up this awful mess!" he says, and kicks a carrot on the floor. It springs up and hits the closet door. "Stay in your rooms until dinner." He leaves the den, slamming the door, making the whole room shake.

Natasha and I quietly gather the carrots and I run to the kitchen to get a sponge for the hummus. Natasha looks at me wide-eyed, an embarrassed smirk on her face. I continue wiping up as if it's no big deal, even though I can hear the blood pulsing in my ears, feel my throat getting tight. But I swallow it back, the thought of crying. I swallow and swallow.

Dinner is quiet. Mom makes vegetable lasagna, which I normally love, but tonight I can barely taste it. Natasha squirms in her seat and eats with her hands until Dad reaches out, brushes her hands away from her mouth, and points to her fork. I concentrate on my food, shoveling in forkful after forkful.

"Mom," I suddenly say, "can I buy lunch at school from now on?"

"Why?" she asks.

"Because everybody does."

She looks at me and chews.

"That's not a great reason," she says.

"Forget it," I say, and try to look really sad.

"I made a new friend today!" Natasha declares.

"That's great, sweetie," Mom says. "What's her name?"

"Jared."

"Oh, a boy," she says.

"Yeah, and he likes more colors than I do."

I slouch and roll my eyes. Now Natasha's off talking about all her strange art stuff that Mom finds so fascinating. For the rest of dinner I know they'll be talking about all the colors of the universe. Natasha loves to paint and draw and she's obsessed with colors, weird ones like fuchsia and lime-green. She actually makes some pretty cool pictures, but I'm not in the mood for Miss Artist and her new color-loving friend.

"Please let me buy lunch tomorrow," I try again. "I won't get any candy. My lunches smell."

"Did someone tell you that?" asks Mom.

"No, they just do. I can smell my tuna from the next room."

"Well, what would you buy?" she says, putting her fork down and leaning back in her chair.

"Chicken nuggets," I say.

"That's it?"

"And an apple."

"You need more than that."

"Pretzels?"

Mom starts eating again and chews slowly on a green pepper from the salad.

"You know it's okay to eat differently from other people if you like what you're eating."

Dad drops his fork onto the plate with an angry clang. We all jump.

"Just let her buy the darn lunch," he says.

Mom glares at him. He keeps his eyes down, picks up his plate, and brings it to the sink. When he's gone, Mom looks at both of us. The corners of her lips twitch up into a faint, embarrassed smile.

"What's wrong with Dad?" Natasha asks.

"He's just having a bad day," Mom says, her lips straight, her voice low.

That night I can't sleep. I creep downstairs long after Mom kisses us both goodnight and stand outside my parents' bedroom. I don't hear the TV, but the light is on. I inch closer to the door, trying not to make a sound. The floorboard creaks. I hold my breath and freeze. After a minute I crane my head to look in the bedroom. I see my dad sitting on the far end of the bed, his back toward me, his face in his hands. Mom's sitting next to him rubbing his back. They're both quiet. Dad probably just misses his job.

The next morning there's a note by my bowl of Cheerios with a five-dollar bill.

Enjoy lunch. Love, Mom

chapter ten

Kate and I sit together at lunch a few days in a row. We get each other laughing about random things, like some boy's funny hat or the way chicken nuggets can actually bounce. Then, on Friday, Jessica, who I've noticed everyone calls Jess, starts to ask questions. She announces over a mouthful of M&M's that her mom said Community is a school for hippies and asks if I'm a hippie, and then says, "What kind of name is Nadha-whatsee anyway?" When I say my name the right way and tell her it's Indian, some boy at the table in back of us pats his mouth and says, "Ahhh, ahhh, ahhh." No, I tell him, calling across my table over to his, not an American Indian, which is what I assume he means when he does that. I'm half Indian, I say, Indian from India.

Then one of the other Jessicas pipes up. "Do you, like, worship cows?" she says, and I say, "No, I'm Jewish." As if that's not enough, another Jessica who calls herself Jess too says, "How can you be Jewish and Indian at the same time? That's really weird." The chicken nuggets I'm chewing start to feel like cardboard and my head gets all floaty like I might rise up off my seat and out of the cafeteria. "You just can," I say, and wish I had a better answer.

Kate keeps quiet during all this. She doesn't join in with the other girls, but she doesn't do anything to help me. She won't even look at me.

The following Monday before lunch I march right up to Alisha while everyone is rushing to the lockers and ask if I can sit with her in the cafeteria. She smiles her calm smile and nods. The kids at her table don't ask annoying questions. They don't ask anything at all. The only person who talks to me is Alisha.

"So you like that Kate girl?" she says as she bites into her bologna sandwich.

"I guess. I don't really know her that well," I say, looking down at my little carton of chicken nuggets. I'm starting to miss my old lunches after having chicken nuggets every day the week before.

"Is she nice?" Alisha asks. "Because some of her friends aren't."

I shrug. "She's pretty nice," I say. Except when all her

friends are asking me awful questions, I almost add, but don't. "But why aren't her friends nice?"

"I don't know. They just don't talk to us. But I guess we don't talk to them."

I assume that by "us" she means the black kids, and "them," the white kids—basically the rest of the school. I want to ask if she considers me an *us* or a *them*. The funny thing is that when I'm with Alisha I want to be an *us*, and when I'm with Kate I want to be a *them*.

"At my old school our class was so small, like a family. Everyone liked each other most of the time," I say, and hope I don't sound like I'm bragging. "It's strange to me how many, um, groups there are here."

Alisha takes this in and nods. She seems to get it.

"Tell me more," she says. "I like to think about it."

I tell her about the day I went grave rubbing and fell in love with Connor O'Reilly. I know I can tell her any story about Community and she'll just listen and like it.

"That's so romantic," she says. Then she asks if she can use it for her book.

"I guess. What's your book about?"

She says it's a romance that takes place in Paris long ago. An innocent man, mistakenly in prison, escapes and hides on a cruise ship from New York to Paris. On the boat he meets a Frenchwoman and falls in love, and they live happily in Paris even though they always have to make sure he's never caught by the police.

I'm so amazed that she could think up such a grown-up idea and write a whole book about it. It must be nice to be able to make up your own world and make people exactly how you want them to be. A journalist doesn't do that. A journalist, Dad says, tries to find out the truth and writes about how things *really* are. That used to seem like an easy thing to do.

"What about your old school?" I ask.

Alisha scratches a sticker off her notebook. "Nothing much to talk about there."

"How come? Was it bad?"

She stops scratching. "No, I was on basketball and softball, which I miss. I don't even think they have a girls' basketball team here. But the classes were really loud and nobody seemed to care much about anything—not the teachers, not the students. I did have one really good teacher and she helped me get here."

"So is Maplewood better?"

She smiles and looks up at me. "It's supposed to be."

chapter eleven

Dad seems to be in a much better mood at dinner that night. He's not in his bathrobe. He makes us steaks on the grill with mashed potatoes and garlic broccoli, probably my most favorite dinner in the universe. He jokes around about his old boss and laughs a lot. He doesn't even get mad when Natasha spills her water, twice. I wonder what cheered him up so much.

After dinner I'm trying to get through my math homework without falling asleep from boredom, when Mom comes upstairs with the cordless phone.

"It's for you," she says, handing me the phone. "Kate."

A nervous warmth spreads over me. "Hey," I say into the phone, trying to sound casual.

"I'm sorry Jess was so mean to you last week," she says.

An "it's okay" slips out of my mouth.

"So I was wondering if you want to try out for cheerleading."

I'm silent; couldn't even speak if I wanted to.

"Sonia?" she asks.

"I've never cheered for anything before."

"Don't worry, most of the girls trying out haven't. It's the first year they've decided to have a sixth-grade team. It usually starts in seventh."

"Have you done it before?"

"I went to cheering camp last summer."

"Oh," I say.

"So I could teach you!" Kate says.

Cheerleading makes me think of bouncy blond high school girls. The kind of girl Kate will probably be when she's older and the kind of girl I don't seem to be at all. But there's something about Kate, besides her blond hair and her mean Jessica friends, that I like. The way we laughed that day together, the way she keeps grabbing my arm in the hallways and whispering secrets in my ears.

"Come on, it'll be fun," she says. "I promise."

"Okay, I'll try out."

"Great! I'm having people over Saturday to practice. Tryouts are in two weeks." Before I know it, I'm taking down her address and phone number.

* * *

"Cheerleading?" Mom says to me when I ask her to drive me there on Saturday. She says it like she's never heard of it before. "For girls your age?"

She's at her desk. The area between her bathroom and bedroom has been her office as long as I can remember, piled so high with paper and books on every surface I'm afraid to sneeze, since the whole thing might come tumbling down. It's her little cave, and lately I can always find her there like a hibernating bear. Come to think of it, Dad's been spending a lot of time in his office too. Maybe that's why my parents always seem tired and grumpy. Maybe they're just working too hard.

"Why not for girls my age?" I say.

"I'm just surprised, that's all. I thought you might like to do something else you're already interested in, like drama. You always loved the plays at Community."

"I'm not at Community anymore."

Mom turns away from me and straightens a stack of papers on her desk. She looks back. "No," she says. "I guess not."

"So will you drive me?"

"Let me think about it." She sighs. "We'll decide in the morning. Go to sleep. It's late." She almost seems to be saying it to herself while she rubs her tired eyes.

The next morning Mom's already gone, teaching an early class. It's the same all week. Mom's added two new classes to her schedule and is busier than I can ever remember her. She doesn't mention cheerleading and neither do I. But I still haven't told Kate I'd show up her house for sure—and it's Friday.

"Whatcha making?" I say to Dad when I get home from school. I try to sound cheerful. He's wearing old sweatpants and a shirt, but he looks like he hasn't showered in a while.

"Pita pizzas," he says as he finishes slicing peppers and mushrooms. He starts on the pepperoni next. The good thing about Dad being home is that we don't have to eat the tofu dishes Mom always made. The bad thing is that I don't know who's doing what anymore, or who I'm supposed to talk to.

"Yum," I say. "Is Mom going to be home soon? I need to ask her something."

"No, it's her night class, remember?" Dad pops a piece of green pepper into his mouth. "You can ask me."

I tell him about Kate and cheering practice. I don't tell him that I already asked Mom.

"Sure. One of us will drive you," he says, without looking up from the cutting board.

Mom comes home late that night and both Natasha and I are already in bed. She pokes her head in the doorway.

"I'm still awake," I say into the darkness.

She stands by the door. "I miss you," she says. Then she comes in and sits on my bed.

"I miss you too," I say, and I do. I don't want to remind her about cheerleading. I just want it to stay all nice and quiet, Mom brushing my hair back from my forehead. "Let's do something together this weekend, just you and me," she says. "Whatever you want." Then she kisses me on the cheek and leaves.

The next morning after breakfast we're all cleaning up dishes when Dad says to Mom, "So I thought I'd drive Sonia to her friend's house later and you can take Natasha to the art store. She said she needs more watercolors." Mom stops scrubbing a pan and looks at me. I pretend a furniture catalog on the counter is the most interesting thing I've ever seen.

"Oh, God, I completely forgot about that. Sonia, why didn't you remind me?"

I clear my throat. I look up. "'Cause Dad said I could go," I say.

"But we hadn't finished talking about it. Why didn't you tell me earlier?" Mom asks Dad.

"Sonia didn't tell me she already asked you," Dad says, and now they're both looking at me with arms crossed. I wish I could transport myself into the catalog and hide away in the lime-green bunk bed.

"I just thought you forgot. I had to tell Kate something," I say.

Mom takes a deep breath. Dad now looks at Mom with arms crossed.

"You could have reminded me," Mom says.

"Well, I didn't want to," I say. My words hang still and strong in the air. "I really want to go and you were going to tell me I couldn't."

"Why would you tell her she couldn't go?" Dad asks as he wipes his hands on a dish towel.

"I'm just not sure cheerleading is appropriate for girls her age," Mom says to Dad like I'm not there. She's back to scrubbing the pan really hard.

"Mom, it's just cheerleading."

"What's wrong with cheerleading?" Dad asks.

Mom just gives a funny sarcastic laugh. "Just turn on any football or basketball game. The girls half naked, shaking their butts, are the cheerleaders."

"Mom, it's not like that," I say.

Mom's face falls and she stops scrubbing again. "You just should have told Dad that you talked to me, that's all." Dad nods in agreement.

"Sorry."

"I didn't know it was that important to you," says Mom in a softer voice.

I didn't know either.

Mom decides to drive me after all, but we don't talk much. When we arrive at Kate's house, Kate and four other girls are jumping around on her green square of a front lawn. I wonder if Mom thinks they look silly, if they look like the girls at the football games on TV. Of course Jess is there, along with three other girls I don't know as well—Christina, a tall skinny girl; Allison, who's shorter, with red curly hair kind of like Sam's; and Ann, who's always smiling and nodding at people.

"I'll pick you up at four," says Mom.

"Yup," I say.

She touches my cheek. "I know it's hard going to a new school, but never forget what a strong, wonderful girl you are. Don't let anyone make you feel less than you are."

"I won't," I say, and get out of the car without looking back.

Kate sees me and waves me over. The other girls say hi and turn their attention back to Kate. She demonstrates a few moves and after a while I find out that the greatest goal a cheerleader can have is to do a perfect toe-touch, a jump where you do a front split in the air and touch your toes. Luckily, I'm pretty flexible. I've done lots of yoga with Mom and can basically bend myself into a pretzel. The girls run through the cheers for tryouts. They all seem to have the word "fight" in them. I'm a little clumsy with the dance moves, but when Kate demonstrates a toe-touch, which she can do well, I know I'll be able to copy her. I try one and my legs cut into the air as if they weigh nothing at all. I slap my sneakered toes so hard it stings the palms of my hands.

"Whoa, Nelly!" says Christina.

All the girls stare at me, even Jess, though she's the only one not smiling.

"That's awesome!" cries Kate and claps really hard. I can't help but feel like a beauty queen. My cheeks must be as red as tomatoes.

I try not to wonder why Kate is so nice to me, and just enjoy it and ignore Jess, who now sits sulkily on the grass painting her toenails hot pink.

For the rest of the afternoon, I do more toe-touches than I'd ever thought I'd do in my life while the other girls try to match my height. After we've all broken a good sweat, Kate suggests a break. Everyone flops on the ground. I lie back for a minute and feel the cold grass tickle my neck.

"Hey, all. Cokes, anyone?" I hear a woman say. I sit up and see Kate's mom, who looks much younger than my mom. Her straight blond hair streams down her back, and she's wearing fitted black pants, a sleeveless white turtleneck, and sunglasses even though it's not that sunny out.

She hands us all cups full of soda. She also has a bag of cheese puffs, which she opens and pokes toward people. After everyone takes a handful, she puts the stuff down on a picnic table on one side of the lawn.

"Hey, Jackie," Jess says, looking up from her nails, which she has gone back to painting.

"Hey, Jess. Nice color," Jackie says. She puts her sunglasses up on her head and thrusts her right hand toward Jess. "What do you think?"

"Ooh, silver. So cool!" Jess squeals.

"Thanks, just got them done," Jackie says, flipping her hair from one shoulder to the other. She looks my way. "You must be Sonia."

"Hi," I say, and immediately want to disappear. All I can think about is my hair, which I don't have tied back, and my scruffy fingernails, and black leggings, and purple T-shirt that aren't anything like the pastel hooded sweat suits all the other girls are wearing.

"Pleased to meet you," she says. "I've heard so much about you!"

To my relief her eyes scan the whole group. "So let's see what you've got, girls." She sits down on one of the picnic table benches. Kate runs over to the middle of the lawn and everyone follows. She leads us through a few cheers and then does a running cartwheel with a toe-touch at the end. Christina and I are the only other girls who attempt it after her.

"Nice one, Sonia," Jackie calls out. The way she sits, leaning back with her long legs crossed, she looks like a movie star.

"That's a real compliment," Kate says. "My mom won a cheering national championship in high school."

"Wow, thanks," I manage, and feel the blood rush to my cheeks again.

Maybe, I think, cheerleading isn't just for other girls. Look at Jess. She's got pink nails and the right sweat suit, but she can't do a toe-touch to save her life.

* * *

For the rest of the week I practice cheers. Natasha is my best audience. I even try to teach her some moves, and the way she stomps through the cheers like a little soldier cracks me up. We tumble on the floor in giggling fits, which is the only thing that seems to get Mom to smile. Otherwise she just watches with her arms crossed, nodding here and there. Once she told me not to shake my butt so much on one of the cheers. When I'm not around her I keep shaking it.

I start sitting with Kate at lunch. Some days I'd rather sit with Alisha, but it seems weird not to sit with Kate since cheerleading has more or less taken over our lives. At least now all the Jessicas leave me alone. But once in a while I see Alisha stealing a glance at me over her notebook in the cafeteria.

The night before tryouts, I know that doing one more toe-touch won't make a difference. My body aches and I've never been so tired, but I can't sleep. I decide to go downstairs and warm some milk in the microwave. Mom says milk has something in it that's supposed to help. If there's anything to worry about, I'll stay up and worry. When I was younger and couldn't sleep, I'd tiptoe into my parents' room to watch them sleep. Dad's a different person when he's sleeping. His face is so still, as if he isn't in his body anymore. Sometimes I'd have to check by opening one of his eyes.

"Dad," I'd ask into his rolled-up eyeball, "are you in there?"

His awake self would snap back into his sleeping body and he'd sit up with a jerk, but he'd never get mad. "I'm always here, even when it seems like I'm not," he'd say, slow and heavy. Then he'd tell me to go back to bed and wait for sleep to find me. "If you lie still enough, it will." And it would, but only after I'd hear him say it.

I think of this now as I creep down the stairs in my T-shirt and bare feet. The door to his study is open a crack and the yellow light of his desk lamp spills out, beckoning me. I push it open, but his desk chair is empty. "Dad?" I whisper. Then I see him on the other side of the room, sleeping on the leather couch in his robe. He breathes deeply and I rest my hand on his stomach. He opens his eyes, but doesn't seem surprised that I'm standing right there.

"Dad?" I whisper again. "Can I tell you something?"

He nods a little.

"I'm trying out for cheerleading tomorrow and I'm going to do every cheer for you."

He stares at me for another second and I wonder if he heard me. Then he smiles and puts his hand on my shoulder before closing his eyes again. I want to ask him why he's sleeping on the couch. To ask him if he misses his old job like I miss Community. But his face goes still again. I watch his chest going up and down, up and down for a few more moments before I head out to the kitchen.

chapter twelve

I eat two bowls of Cheerios to give me extra energy for try-outs. Mom rushes around, making sure she has her phone, her keys, her big black bag stuffed with her laptop, and the right books, and kisses me on the forehead. She whispers in my ear a tight "good luck" and then she's out the door. My stomach churns as I listen to the back door close and her car tires rolling out on the gravel. When I bolt out the door for the bus, Dad calls after me with Natasha by his side.

"Sonia!"

I stop halfway down the driveway and turn around.

"I'll cheer for you today too," he says, and gives me a thumbs-up. Natasha yells, "Go, Sonia!" and tries to do a toe-touch, but only manages to hit her knees.

I laugh, give them a thumbs-up back, and run the rest of the way.

* * *

At school the morning drags. I can practically hear the clock ticking. Kate throws me a note in the middle of Mrs. Langley's grammar lesson.

> You're going to do so awesome today. I just know it!
>
> XXXOOO,
>
> Kate

I'm about to fling a note back to her that says *So will you!*, with only one set of *xo*s because I'm not ready to hug and kiss Kate three times, when Mrs. Langley calls my name.

"Sonia," she says, her back still turned as she writes on the board. "Come here, please."

I suck in my breath. I've never gotten in trouble at school before. Once in a while Jack had to tell me and Sam to stop talking, but that was it. What I know is this—Mrs. Langley gives detentions for passing notes in class. I'm not sure what goes on during a detention, but I've seen other kids get them and they don't look happy about it. I imagine them being sent down into a dusty dungeon where Mrs. Langley forces them to memorize thousands of vocabulary words.

With all eyes on me, I go up to her desk.

"May I have the note, please," she says, thrusting out her hand, wiggling her fingers. I hand it over.

"This is the only warning I'm giving you. Next time, detention," she says. Then she rips up my note and throws it into the garbage. I stand there for a second, wondering if people can see my heart pounding through my shirt.

"Please return to your seat," she says, turning to face the board again. Mrs. Langley must really have eyes in the back of her head. Walking back to my desk on shaky legs, I wonder if Mrs. Langley's actually a robot.

At the end of the day Kate and Jess wait for me by the lockers and we all go into the gym together. Jess smiles at me. A first.

"You're so lucky you didn't get detention. You would've missed tryouts," she says while she chews on the corner of her thumbnail.

"Yeah," says Kate. "I would have felt *so* bad."

I give her a small laugh and shrug.

"It's no big deal, though," Jess says.

"What's no big deal?" I ask her.

"Detention. I've had two. She just makes you copy words out of the dictionary for a half hour."

"Oh, you're such a juvenile delinquent," Kate says to Jess, and pokes her in the shoulder. Then they crack up.

"Just remember I was the one who pretended they were

my notes. Basically I did your detentions," Jess says. Kate smiles a funny lopsided smile and quickly looks down.

"I know, I owe you," she says, and pats Jess on the back. Jess beams.

I sit cross-legged on the gym floor while the eighth-grade cheerleading captain explains the rules. The seventh- and eighth-grade cheerleading captains are judging our tryouts, along with Mr. Totono, the gym teacher. Everyone is supposed to do two cheers, a toe-touch, and a cartwheel split. Kate is asked to go first, since her last name is Anderson. She stands fearlessly tall in front of the judges with her hands on her hips, waiting for the signal to go. They nod to her and she starts, her face glowing, her voice ricocheting off the gym walls. Her moves are sharp and strong.

I can tell the judges love her, the way they stare hard and smile. When she's done they clap and I wonder if they'll clap for everyone. Kate bounds back to her place in between me and Jess and grabs our hands. "You were great," I say, squeezing her hand. A few more girls go and the judges clap, but not in the same way. Then it's Jess's turn. She stands up and starts before she's told to. She goes through the cheers quickly, without smiling, and doesn't even touch her toes during her jump. At the end she smiles and sticks out her chest. The judges clap politely. When Jess sits back down Kate gives her a hug. I smile and hope that maybe Jess won't make the team, but then I remember that Mom always says that if you wish mean things on other people, bad energy will come back to you. My stomach does a flip knowing my turn is coming up. I just try to focus on what Dad said this morning.

The eighth-grade captain stumbles through my last name. Mr. Totono corrects her. She says it one more time incorrectly, "Nah-da-da-hoomy," gives me a squinty glance, and gestures for me to begin. Not a good start. But Mr. Totono smiles his electric smile, which helps. I imagine that the judges are my old class at Community. I see Jack, Sam, and Connor cheering, clapping, whistling two-fingered whistles. I get through the cheers well enough, but my voice isn't as loud and my moves aren't as sharp as Kate's. Then it's time for the toe-touch. I wind up and go for it.

When I sit down, my hands sting from the jump. The judges look pleased. Kate turns to me and squeezes my arm.

I squeeze her back and see Jess out of the corner of my eye, looking down at her feet, knocking her toes together over and over.

chapter thirteen

I have to wait a whole week to find out who made the team and every day feels twice as long. On Thursday after school, while we're waiting for our buses, I tell Alisha how nervous I am. "I'm sure you made it," she says in a distracted way.

Then she quickly changes the subject. "Have you ever been to India?" she asks me.

"I went two years ago," I tell her. "I saw where my father grew up."

"What was it like there?" she asks, eyes wide.

"Hot and colorful. There are flowers everywhere and the scent of spices and incense fills the air. But some people smell bad. Especially on the train. My favorite thing was the Taj Mahal." I explain what the Taj Mahal is, how a king had twenty thousand people build this huge mausoleum for his wife, who died giving birth to their fourteenth child. It took the builders twenty-two years to finish it. I tell her about the flower designs in the marble tiles made out of millions of little jewels and how I couldn't stop staring at them, how I couldn't believe it took forty or fifty jewels just to make a petal on one of the flowers.

"Talk about romantic," Alisha says. "I should put something about the Taj Mahal in my book. The farthest I've ever been is Disney World. We drove all the way to Florida once. Have you been anywhere else?"

I tell her I've been to see my cousins in Israel too.

"I can't believe you've been to France, India, and Israel already. You're so lucky," she says. I've never thought about the fact that traveling is lucky. I just thought some people did and some people didn't. But I guess it's a pretty expensive thing to do.

"What's it like being Jewish?" she asks.

"I'm not really the best person to ask," I say. I think of Sam and how she could tell Alisha all about her temple and Shabbat and the meaning of every holiday.

"Why not?"

"We're not that religious."

"Oh," Alisha says, then starts playing with a small hole on the thigh of her jeans. She seems disappointed that I don't have more to say. But the most Jewish thing that happens in my house is lighting the menorah on Hanukkah. My dad is technically Hindu, but isn't religious at all and just sort of goes along with the Jewish holidays. He'll put a yarmulke on at my grandparents' Passover seder, but the way he sits at the table, arms crossed, an empty look on his face, is part of what makes me feel only half Jewish. The same way that my grandparents bickering in Yiddish the way they do, or how light my mom's skin is, how green her eyes are, makes me feel half Indian. For everything that reminds me of who I am, there's always something reminding me of who I'm not.

"Do you feel more Indian or Jewish?" Alisha asks with her usual serious voice and piercing stare, like she can read my mind. Alisha sure likes to ask questions. Maybe she should be a journalist. I look down and see my brown toes poking through my sandals. They look just like Dad's toes, the second one a little longer than my big toe, and they're almost as brown. My toes look Indian. So does the rest of me. My name sounds Indian. There really isn't anything about me that's Jewish—at least, not anything anyone could see.

"If you had to choose," she says.

I just stand there with my mouth partly open.

Alisha's bus pulls up. "Tell me tomorrow," she says. "Hey, do you want to come over after school? You can ride home with me on the bus. It's really not that far away. The bus just takes a while."

"Oh," I say, surprised. It sort of seemed easier to have our friendship right here waiting for the bus, separate from class, separate from our houses, separate from Kate. "Let me check with my parents." Her face changes from happy to serious. "I just need to make sure someone can pick me up." She smiles again and I notice my heart's beating a little faster. I wipe my sweaty hands on my jeans.

"Okay, call me tonight," she says, and runs up the steps of her blue and white bus.

Maybe it would be easier to just be Indian and not have to explain the Jewish part. Mom doesn't seem to think being Jewish is that important, otherwise she would have done all the things Sadie does—belong to a temple, have Shabbat dinner every Friday night, and send me to Hebrew school. Why didn't she do those things for me? Why couldn't she have raised me really Jewish like Sam, so I wouldn't have to think so much about it? Now it's too late.

When I get home I skip watching SpongeBob with Natasha and go to the phone in the kitchen. I hold the receiver until my hand gets stiff. I finally dial and Sam answers. We haven't talked in two weeks, the longest we've ever gone since we've known each other.

"I knew you'd call me today," she says.

I want to ask why she hasn't called me, but I don't. "Tell me everything I've missed," I say.

She sighs. "I don't know. It's kind of hard to remember."

"You can remember one thing, can't you?"

"One thing. One thing," she repeats, thinking. "Okay, how about this: Jack picked me to be the lead in the play this year."

"Wow, that's so great," I say, feeling hurt. "How come you didn't tell me?"

There's silence on the other end for a second. She clears her throat.

"I just found out," she finally says, but that doesn't answer my question, or at least answer it in the way I want it answered. "So what's going on with you? Have you made lots of new friends?" Her voice sounds squeaky.

"A few, I guess. I tried out for cheerleading."

"Cheerleading?" she says, and laughs.

"What's so funny?"

"I just can't picture you as a cheerleader."

"Why?" I ask. "I'm pretty good at it."

"Do you have to wear some silly uniform?"

"I don't know if I've even made the team." I hadn't thought much about the uniform and whether it would be silly. "I'd better go, I've got a lot of homework," I lie. But Sam lied too. She said it wouldn't happen to us.

All through dinner, the conversation with Sam sits like a rock in my stomach, along with the half-burned meat loaf Dad made. I eat the salad and rice and push the slice of brown mush around my plate. Dad is talking about the news.

"This country's in trouble," he says. "Big trouble." I want to ask him why, but I don't. It scares me the way he says it, like he knows all these important secrets about the world that nobody else knows. Then he starts talking fast about gas prices, and terrorism, and the downturn in the economy.

Many times Mom and Dad will debate what they heard on the news like a game of Ping-Pong. It's fun to listen to them even if I don't understand what they're talking about. But now it's like he's talking to the air. Mom nods at him, but she doesn't try to argue with what he's saying. Her eyes squint like something's hurting her. Natasha takes a big bite of her meat loaf, chews it up, and shows it to me.

"Ick!" I shriek. Dad stops talking and jumps as if someone just slapped him. Normally Mom would tell Natasha to stop it, but instead she says quickly, "Sonia, how are you feeling about cheerleading? You'll see the tryout results tomorrow, right?"

"I feel good," I say, and put my fork down. I didn't think she had any idea that I would find out tomorrow.

"Well, all that matters is that you tried," she says, looking off into the distance.

"Whatever," I say.

"What's that supposed to mean?" Mom says, and suddenly looks sad. Her eyes are watery, like she might cry. I feel bad for her. Nobody's been very nice to her lately, but then again, she hasn't been that nice either.

"I *want* to make it. I'm really good, believe it or not, and it does matter to me."

"That's not what I meant, I just meant it's good that you tried even if you don't make it."

"No, it's not good! It'll suck."

I said it. I said the word that Mom and Dad hate more than anything. In my house it's even worse than the other S-word and maybe even the F-word, even though I never dare to say them.

Mom opens her mouth to say something, but Dad gets up fast, takes my dinner into the kitchen, and throws the whole thing, plate and all, into the garbage. He points upstairs and says through gritted teeth, "You can eat when you decide to show your mom some respect. I don't want to see you again tonight." I get up on shaky legs, feeling the rest of my family's eyes on my back, watching me. I go up to my room and curl up into a ball on my bed.

Later that night, I can hear Mom getting Natasha ready for bed and the soft sounds of her reading *Where the Wild Things Are* through my closed door.

After a little while there's a knock at my door. She comes in with Natasha, which is kind of weird.

"I'm sorry, Mom," I say, tears flooding my eyes. I am sorry, yet I meant what I said, even the "suck" part.

"Me too," she says. "We haven't been connecting well lately. It's my fault." She sits in my desk chair, takes off her glasses, and starts cleaning them. Natasha plops down on the floor. "Things have been hard for all of us, and we should talk about it." Her voice cracks slightly. I know what I'm about to hear is bad. I know it the way you can see a thunderstorm coming, in the darkening sky, in the *whoosh* of wind rustling the trees.

She clears her throat. "Remember when I said Dad was going through a difficult time?" she continues.

"Yeah," I say.

"Is he sick?" asks Natasha.

"Well, there are different kinds of sick," Mom says. Then she goes on to explain what's wrong with Dad, how it's sort of like having a flu in your mind, that he's been feeling down for a while, and when bad moods last too long it's called a depression.

"Your father is depressed, girls."

"When will he feel better?" Natasha asks.

"Soon. He's seeing a doctor who will help him. A therapist," Mom says, and rubs her face the way she does when she's tired, like her whole face itches all over. Then she stops rubbing. "I promise it's going to be okay. And you can ask me anything you want."

"Does this mean he's not going to get a new job?" I ask, hoping Mom means I really can ask anything I want.

"Eventually." Mom puts her fingers on her forehead like she has a headache. "Dad has been depressed before, but this time it's a little worse. His doctor will help him through it, and as soon as he's feeling better, he'll find another job. In the meantime, I'm going to have to work more."

I take a deep breath in and let it out slowly. I try to think about other times I've seen Dad like this, but I can't.

"When was he depressed?" I ask.

"A long time ago, before you were born," Mom says. "But please don't talk about it with other people. Dad needs his privacy. We all do."

Natasha climbs on my bed. Mom comes over and puts her arms around us. We sit quietly for a little while until all I want to think about—all I *can* think about—is sleep finding me.

She kisses me on the cheek and says softly, "I'm sure you blew the judges away." Then she leads Natasha out of my room.

I never ask if I can go over to Alisha's house.

chapter fourteen

When the tryout results are posted on Friday afternoon, I see a crowd of twenty or so girls looking for their names on the list in the girls' locker room. I watch Kate run up to the list, bounce on her toes, and clap her hands. I watch Jess look at it, squeal, and hug Kate. I watch some other girls look at it, hang their heads, and walk away. I watch Christina, the girl I met at Kate's house, look at it and start crying. I push my way to the front. Kate comes up out of nowhere and puts an arm around my shoulders. My eyes scan the list. I don't see my name, and I swallow hard to make sure not one tear sneaks out. Then way at the bottom I see two names. One is mine. It says in bold capital letters SONIA NADHAMUNI—ALTERNATE. "Alternate." It's a word I've never really heard of before, in the sense that someone could be one. Yet I am.

I'm not sad, I'm not happy. I'm an alternate.

"What does it mean?" I ask Kate.

"It means you're totally on the team!" she says, hugging me.

I see Jess and some other girls who've made it huddle around one another, talking fast with flushed faces. I was better than Jess, way better. I was better than most of those girls, maybe not Kate, but better than most. Maybe it doesn't just have to do with how good you are. Those girls aren't new. They have names everyone can pronounce. They know exactly which lunch table they belong at.

"But how is it different?" I ask Kate.

"Don't worry. I'm captain, and as far as I'm concerned, you're on the team just like anyone else," she says. Then she grabs my arm and thrusts me into the circle of the other giggling cheerleaders. Their voices blur into one shriek of excitement, one high-pitched sound that rings in my ears.

I find out later from the other alternate, Ann, what it really means. It means I can practice with everyone, but I only cheer in the games when one of the real cheerleaders can't make it, which is probably not very often. Ann doesn't seem upset by this, so I pretend I'm not either and stand with my hands in my pockets with a stiff smile on my face. I'm half Indian, I'm half Jewish, and now I'm half a cheerleader.

I've avoided eye contact with Alisha all day, but here I am waiting for my bus with no escape. She comes up to me, but before she even says anything, I tell her why I didn't call her.

"I kind of got into a fight with my parents last night and I never asked them about coming over. I'm sorry," I say.

"Was the fight about coming over to my house?" she asks.

"What? No. Why would you think that?"

"I don't know," Alisha says, and walks off to where her bus pulls up.

I trudge off to my own bus and wonder if Alisha will ever want me over again.

At home nobody rushes to ask me if I've made the team or not. Natasha is locked in her room again, banging on her drums louder than I've ever heard her. Mom is busy making dinner, and for once I'm happy to see her cooking even if she's preparing something with lots of tofu and spinach to make up for lost time. Dad's outside in his navy blue bathrobe sweeping leaves off the patio.

It's strange how robes and pajamas can seem so cozy at the right times and so sad at the wrong times. I open the sliding glass door and feel a surprising chill in the air. It smells like cold dirt, like snow about to fall, like winter.

"Can I help?" I ask him.

He turns around and then I see it, the cigarette in his mouth, the smoke in the air, curling around his head. He might as well be naked. I've never seen him smoke. I didn't even know he did. I wonder what other things I don't know about my dad. A quick sweat breaks out on my forehead. I grip the doorframe to steady myself.

He holds out his broom to me, sits down on the picnic bench, and presses the cigarette into the stone patio until it's out. I begin sweeping fast. I want to finish and leave this stranger smoking on our patio.

"Did you make the team?" he asks.

I stop sweeping and watch as the last of the smoke curls out of his mouth. Through the haze I catch a glimpse of my old father with his crow-eyed smile.

"I only made it as an alternate," I say, and wonder if he'll know what I mean. I cough a little with my mouth tightly closed.

"Are you happy about that?" he asks.

"I'm not sure."

"It's better to be an alternate than nothing at all. Nothing's worse than being nothing. Remember that, Sonia," he says.

"Okay," I say. "Dad?"

"What?"

I want to ask why he's smoking, if he feels depressed right now, if he feels like nothing. "I'm going to see if Mom needs help with dinner," I say instead.

"Good," he says, holding out his hand to take the broom back, and I let him have it. I walk away and close the glass door behind me. When I'm far enough away from the door I turn around. His back is facing me. The broom is propped up against the picnic table. He's crouched over a bit, the smoke once more rising above him. I don't go into the kitchen to help Mom. I go into my room and start on my homework even though it's Friday.

On Monday morning Dad's in a suit drinking coffee and rushing around the kitchen. Mom hands me a plate of scrambled eggs and wheat toast. I take it and sit down across from Natasha. We both stare at our parents over steaming plates of food.

"Hey," Natasha whispers.

I take in her big brown eyes and dark floppy hair that Mom has given up trying to control. I forget sometimes how little she still is. In fact, the way she looks now, with her cheeks rosy and big, I can remember what she looked like when she wore diapers. I suddenly want to hold her hand and sing to her like Mom used to let me do when she slept in a crib.

"Yeah?" I whisper back.

"Is Dad better now?" she asks.

"Maybe," I say, and hold out my hand flat on the table so she can slap me five.

Dad's talking to Mom by the stove. His eyes are bright and flashing. At one point Mom reaches over and straightens his tie. Then he comes over to the table with his plate and crunches on his toast while glancing at the paper.

"I want you both to have a fantastic day," he says, and stands up and kisses us each on the forehead. Then he's out the door like lightning, as if I imagined the whole thing.

"Mom?" Natasha asks when he's gone. "Does Dad have a new job?"

"No, but he has a job interview," she says, and I can see from the twitching corners of her mouth that she's trying not to smile.

In the afternoon I have my first cheerleading practice by the bleachers near the football field. I tell Mom just as I'm running out for the bus, just kind of yell it out to her, that I'm taking the late bus home because of practice. Her shoulders fall.

"I'm so sorry I forgot to ask," she says, but that's all. She doesn't say she's happy for me. She doesn't say "good job" or "good luck," or anything like that. Maybe I'll become a professional cheerleader, so she'll finally have to admit that I'm good at it and that cheerleading is okay.

chapter fifteen

When I get to the track near the bleachers, not everyone is there yet. Kate, Jess, and a few other girls crowd together and gossip about the football players who are practicing out on the field. I walk up to them and stand beside Kate. Jess is still trying to convince Kate that Peter Hanson likes her.

"He's so looking at you," Jess says, and glances sideways at the players. They're completely covered in gear, including helmets. I wonder how Jess even knows who Peter is, let alone sees him looking at Kate. Kate turns boldly in the boys' direction. "He so *isn't,* and I'm not really into him anyway," she says, but a blush on her cheeks makes me think she cares more than she lets on. He's one of the tallest boys in our class and he is pretty cute, I have to admit, but he's always surrounded by a bunch of boys who like to talk loudly and punch each other in the arms. In my opinion no boy could come close to Connor O'Reilly, the most beautiful boy I've ever seen. Connor is a lot different from the boys here. He can draw really well and play the guitar. Sometimes he and Jack would do duets together during lunch. I'm not used to arm-punching, football-playing boys like Peter Hanson. We didn't have sports teams at Community. We'd run races or play soccer or basketball during recess, but that was it.

Finally when all the girls arrive we sit on the grass and Kate starts to run the practice. First she takes down everyone's size for uniforms and asks for a show of hands of who wants sneakers and who wants saddle shoes. I have no idea what saddle shoes look like, so when Kate first asks who wants sneakers, I raise my hand. I'm the only one. The other girls sneak sideways glances at me while Kate writes something in her notebook.

"Okay," she says. "Before we start warming up, I want to tell you some stuff. First"—she pauses to run her hand down her golden braid—"I'm so psyched about this team. We're the youngest squad in the county and that's really awesome." A few girls yell out a "whoo-hoo!" "And second, as captain, I've decided to cut out the alternates."

I look at her in shock. I make my hands into fists, dig my nails into my palms. Fine, she's throwing us off the team in front of everyone else. Fine. Fine. Fine. I always knew there was something about Kate I couldn't trust. Maybe she just thought it would be fun to mess with my head. Mom will probably be thrilled.

"Including the alternates, we have ten people on the team," Kate continues while she paces back and forth in her pink sweats. "The seventh-grade team has ten people, not including alternates. So I've decided that Sonia and Ann should be regular members of the team and cheer at all games. If someone's sick, we'll just change the pyramids last minute. Sound cool?" She says this loud and strong, in true cheerleader style.

Before I know what's happening Ann comes over and gives me a quick hug. Some of the other girls clap. I catch Jess's eye and she quickly looks away. My hands tingle and a smile spreads slowly across my face.

After practice Kate asks me to have dinner at her house.

"I guess that's all right," Mom says when I call her from the pay phone in the gym. "Pick you up at eight."

Kate pulls on my elbow. "Ask her if you can sleep over," she says. The thought of not having to return to my nervous mom and sad dad and confused little sister sounds pretty good.

"Can I sleep over?"

"On a school night?" Mom says.

"I don't have any homework," I lie. "Please."

There's silence on the other end for a second. "Are you sure it's all right with Kate's parents?" Mom asks.

I cover the phone. "Is it all right with your parents?"

Kate nods.

"Yes," I say.

To my relief, Mom doesn't bother to ask how Kate knows this, but from the impression I got from Jackie, Kate probably has school-day sleepovers all the time.

"What are you going to do for clothes, a toothbrush, lunch?" Mom asks.

"I'll borrow stuff from Kate." Kate nods vigorously while I say this. "She says it's fine."

By some strange miracle Mom lets me.

The bus trip to Kate's house is much shorter than mine. She could actually walk to school, but since it would be along a very busy road her parents don't let her. We go in the back door and Kate throws her backpack down in the corner of the small kitchen. I put mine next to hers.

"In the closet, please," Jackie says, pointing to the backpacks. She stands over a round wooden table, arranging a vase filled with yellow roses. She's wearing a pair of tight jeans, a lacy white T-shirt, and sequined pink flip-flops. She looks cooler than most of the teenagers in my town.

Kate takes our backpacks and hangs them in the coat closet. Then she starts hunting through the fridge. I stuff my hands in my jeans pockets and watch Jackie fiddle with the roses.

"There's some ham and Swiss in there. Hey, Sonia," she

says, flashing me a quick sparkly smile. I like the way Jackie says "hey" rather than "hi." It makes me feel like she knows me better than she does.

"Hi," I say, giving her a little wave. "Thanks for having me over."

Kate grabs some ham, cheese, a loaf of pumpernickel bread, and a jar of mayonnaise and sets up on the kitchen counter. I've never had a ham sandwich in my life. I don't tell this to Kate. I help her, hoping she thinks I eat ham sandwiches every day. Kate's probably never had non-meat meat loaf either. We both make a sandwich and she pours me a glass of Coke. Then she takes her plate and her Coke, stuffs a can of Pringles—another thing I've never eaten—under her arm, and starts for the living room. I follow her.

"Don't eat too much, we're going to Rudy's tonight," Jackie calls after us.

"We won't," Kate calls back. We both sit cross-legged on the couch. I take a bite of my sandwich. It's salty and full of mayonnaise and wonderful, topped only by a handful of Pringles and a sip of cold Coke.

"Have you been to Rudy's? We go there all the time."

"Yeah," I say, and I'm relieved that though I'm new to the world of ham sandwiches and Pringles, I have been to the neighborhood Italian restaurant, Rudy's. But only a few times. Mom thinks it's too greasy.

Kate pops a couple of chips into her mouth and grabs the

remote. We both settle in on the puffy tan couch. Everything in Kate's home looks like it's out of a magazine. A thick, colorful rug sits under the coffee table and the wooden floors shine. There are fresh white roses in a vase over the fireplace. I'm surprised that Jackie lets Kate eat in here. Mom never lets us eat in the living room, the one fancy room in our house. Everything else in our house is sort of crowded and mismatched. There are shelves everywhere stuffed with books and knickknacks. And most of our furniture comes from all the countries my parents have traveled to. Our living room is all from Japan. Our dining room table is from Mexico. And we have lots of pillows and rugs from India all over the house. There's even one little rug with a big hole in it in the kitchen from the house Dad grew up in.

Kate turns on what she says is her favorite reality show. It's about a woman who has to choose a husband out of a bunch of men. She walks around and talks to them in a really sparkly pink dress. Two of the men get into an argument about who has spent more time talking to the woman. Then one man pushes the other into a pool. If there's one thing Mom hates more than anything, more than junk food, more than cheerleading, it's reality TV.

I hear Jackie's flip-flops flip-flopping down the hallway. "Do you guys want to go to the mall?" She asks, poking her head into the living room with her sunglasses on, twirling her car keys. "I have to return some shoes." Kate quickly jumps up and turns off the TV. "Sure," she says, and off we go.

The mall, a place where Mom drags me and Natasha for new school clothes, sneakers, or bathing suits a few times a year, is a very different place with Kate and Jackie. First we head to the shoe store, not the sporty discount one we always go to, but a nicer one that has about thirty different kinds of shoes displayed like pieces of art on glass shelves. The way Kate and Jackie walk around intensely gazing at the shoes, pausing to focus on one particular pair, reminds me of a show I once saw about lions hunting their prey. I follow them, afraid to touch anything. Jackie finally pounces on a shiny pair of red flats with very pointy toes.

"Like?" she asks Kate, holding up the shoe. Kate walks over and takes the shoe from her mother and turns it this way and that. I wonder what she's looking for.

"Yes," Kate says. Then she shows Jackie a pair of black patent leather sandals. They both huddle around the shoes and discuss their good and bad qualities. Kate decides to put them down.

Just for something to do, I go over and look at a pair of green loafers. The green reminds me of grass in the spring. I run my finger down the fronts of them; I've never felt leather so soft.

"Those are cool. They're totally you," Kate says behind me.

"Really?" I say, and wonder what I have in common with

a pair of green loafers. I pick one up and turn it over: eighty dollars, says the price sticker in thick red marker. I've never had a pair of shoes that cost more than thirty.

"Try them on." Kate holds up the shoe in the direction of the saleswoman. I'm about to stop her, but it's too late.

"Size?" the woman asks.

"Seven?" I say in a quiet voice, and drop myself into one of the black leather chairs.

The saleswoman comes back, kneels down in front of me, and takes off my beat-up sneakers. I'm afraid my feet smell, but she doesn't seem to care or notice. The shoes fit like gloves.

"They look great, Sonia," Kate says, and Jackie, who's come over, agrees. I think I'm starting to catch what they have—shoe fever. I picture myself walking into the cafeteria with my green shoes on. The other girls in my class shower me with compliments. Even the boys stare. My chin lifts and my heart swells at the thought. But they're eighty dollars. I have a dollar fifty in my pocket. *Bang. Crash. Boom.*

Jackie must notice my face fall. "My treat," she tells me.

I know I can't let her and yet these green loafers have suddenly become everything I've ever wanted.

"No, you don't have to do that," I say, not all that convincingly. But when it comes to shoes, Jackie doesn't need much convincing. She whips out her credit card and hands it to the saleswoman along with her red flats.

"Wear them out of the store," Kate says. And I do. I can't stop looking at my feet. When I walk out of the mall, it feels like the whole world is admiring me.

"Hiya, pumpkin," Kate's dad says to her as we all come through the kitchen door. He's sitting at the kitchen table, his feet up on another chair, reading the paper. He wears jeans and a T-shirt and a tool belt around his waist. He's tall, with spiky brown hair, and his green eyes practically have Christmas lights in them. He's one of the best-looking men I've ever seen. He's as much of a non-dad dad as Jackie is a non-mom mom. I can't believe I'm thinking this about Kate's dad.

Kate walks over to him, and he grabs her around the waist and gives her a quick squeeze. She pats his head.

"Dad, I think you need a haircut."

"Holy green shoes!" he says, looking at me.

"Dad, this is Sonia. Aren't they the coolest?"

"Pleased to meet you, Sonia. I'm Greg and those"—he points down—"are rockin' shoes." I smile and quickly look to where he's pointing so that he won't see me blush.

Then Jackie comes marching into the kitchen after bringing her shopping bags upstairs and flings herself into Greg's lap. He grabs her and she gives him a not-so-small kiss on the mouth.

"Ugh, come on," Kate says, and grabs my arm.

"We're leaving for dinner in fifteen minutes," Jackie calls.

It's close to eight. My family never has dinner on a school night past seven. And we only go out on the weekends.

I follow Kate up to her room. It's like living inside a doll's house. It's small and perfect. The bed reminds me of a cake—fluffy, white, and pink, decorated with tons of pillows. Paper patterned with little roses covers the walls. Silver-framed photos gleam on top of a heavy wooden dresser. There's a pink-and-green-painted desk in the corner. It's also incredibly neat. I didn't know anyone my age was this neat.

She opens up a very organized closet and takes out a fuzzy white and green sweater.

"This will go perfectly with your shoes," she says, and hands it to me. I dutifully put it on. It smells of lavender. Then she takes a lipstick out of her dresser drawer and pokes it in my direction. I take it from her and smooth on the frosty pink shade. Mom says I have to wait until I'm in high school to wear lipstick, but she isn't here in this room, in this sweater, in these green shoes. I look in Kate's mirror and like what I see.

chapter sixteen

The next day I wear the sweater, shoes, and lipstick to school and Kate's mom gives us both lunch money. All day I get compliments on my shoes. Even Alisha says she likes them while we're waiting after school for the bus, and she's not the type to care about shoes. Alisha always wears the same thing to school—jeans, sneakers, and a black or gray T-shirt.

Then she says, "You're starting to look like her," and frowns a little.

"Is that bad?" I laugh, because I couldn't look like Kate in a million years, no matter what I wore.

"It depends," she says in her matter-of-fact way.

"On what?" I start biting away on my thumbnail.

"On what you want to look like. You looked fine to me before," she says, and shrugs. Things have been weird with me and Alisha. She hasn't mentioned coming over to her house again and I haven't either. Maybe I just want to concentrate on Kate and cheerleading right now. Maybe that's enough.

Then Alisha reaches in her jeans pocket and fishes out a shiny green rock.

"Look, it's jade," she says. "Same color as your shoes." She gives it to me. I turn the rock around in my hand. It's cool and smooth. It makes me feel good just holding it. When her bus comes I close my hand tight around the rock.

"Can I have it back?" she asks, and holds out her hand.

"Yeah," I say, but I don't want to let it go. She wiggles her fingers and I finally press it into her palm. My hand looks so light next to hers I almost don't recognize myself.

Out of the corner of my eye I see Kate and Jess walk past us to Kate's bus. Jess is talking fast and loud about something and doesn't see us. At first I think they're going to walk by without even saying hi, but then Kate looks up and gives me a low little wave, as if she doesn't want Jess to see. I wave back the same way and think about what we would all look like standing together, Alisha on one side, Kate on the other, me in the middle. Like a pen running out of ink.

"What are those things on your feet?" Mom asks when I get home. It takes about three seconds for her to notice the green loafers.

"Shoes," I say without looking at her. I go over to the fridge and hunt for a snack. All I see is soy milk, a bag of carrots, cauliflower, and some goat cheese. I close the fridge and open the pantry. Pretzels and a cranberry juice box will have to do.

"How come we never have any good food in this house?"

"Please don't talk to me that way." Mom looks at me with her hands on her hips. "Are they Kate's?"

"Kind of," I say.

I hear the *thud, thud, thud* of my heart, so I grab a handful of pretzels and stuff them into my mouth. I can't answer her if my mouth is full. She stares at me, waiting. The pretzels taste like sawdust.

"Sonia, what's going on?" she asks. Her eyebrows scrunch together in her sort of angry, sort of worried way.

"Nothing," I say, and take a swig of juice to clear away the last of the pretzels. "Jackie bought them for me."

"Kate's mother?" she says, and starts sorting the mail piled on the counter. I look at Mom's clunky black clogs that she wears every day, at her frizzy salt-and-pepper hair clamped back with an old silver barrette, at her gray pants and black sweater she's had for years. Boy, does she need a makeover.

"Uh-huh," I say with a nod.

She stops sorting the mail and looks at me through her thick brown-framed glasses. Then she looks down at the shoes.

"How much were they?"

I want to stuff the whole bag of pretzels into my mouth.

"Forty dollars," I lie.

"First of all," Mom says, gesturing with a piece of mail, "if you need new things, just tell me. And forty dollars is a lot to spend on a pair of such impractical shoes."

If only she could see Kate and Jackie's shoe collections. "Mom, I've been wearing the same pair of sneakers forever."

"Just talk to me about it first, Sonia," she says, and grabs her purse. "Here, please pay Jackie back."

I fold and unfold the crisp twenty-dollar bills. Money is a strange thing. My family has a bigger house than Kate, three cars, and has been to places all over the world. And I used to go to private school. All those things cost a lot of money. Kate's never been anywhere far away and her house is small, but it looks nicer than ours. They go out to dinner all the time and spend eighty dollars on shoes like it's nothing, things my family never does. Dad used to have a fancy office and probably made a good amount of money. Mom makes money too. Kate's dad is a carpenter and Jackie doesn't work. But they act like they have a lot more money than we do. Maybe they do, somehow. I really don't get it.

At dinner, Dad looks happier than I've seen him in a long time.

"All right, everyone," he says as soon as we're all sitting down to tofu-broccoli lasagna—one of Mom's better tofu creations. At least it has real cheese melted on top. "You're looking at the new sales director for Riley Publishing," he says, and leans back in his chair with his arms crossed. Mom looks sparkly and proud. It all seems to be moving so fast. Based on what Mom said last week, I thought Dad was going to be home for a long time.

"Hooray!" Natasha shouts while she twirls a long piece of melted cheese around her fork. "But what's Riley Publishing?"

"It's another company that publishes textbooks, just like the one I worked at before but bigger."

"Do you sell them outside?" Natasha asks.

Something settles over Dad's face, something cloudy, something dark.

"The books?" he says.

"Yeah, do you sell them outside or in a store? Because our school had a book sale and we sold them outside."

"Well, this is different. I work for a company that makes books and I figure out what other businesses and schools we're going to sell them to."

"Oh," she says over a big mouthful. I can see the green, red, and white food churning around in her mouth. "Selling them outside is better if it's a sunny day. Not if it rains, though."

"Natasha, I want you to understand my job," Dad says. His voice is low and impatient. "I work for a big company that makes books for people who need to learn important things." He gestures with his fork, poking at the air. "It's much different from a book sale at your school."

Mom, who's moving the hair out of Natasha's eyes, stops and shoots Dad an angry glare. "Well, both ways of selling books are important," she says in a way that means he'd better agree, and fast.

"I just want her to understand what her father does," he says. Mom opens her mouth to say something, then closes it again and shakes her head. She goes back to fixing Natasha's hair, but Natasha brushes her hand away.

"So you're not sick anymore?" Natasha says to Dad.

I stare at Dad. Then my parents look at each other and back at Natasha. Mom rubs her face. Dad looks down at his plate.

Dad looks up. "I am feeling better," he says in the same low voice, but it doesn't sound like he believes what he's saying. Mom nods.

"I think your job sounds great, Dad," I say. The clouds on his face pass. He looks at me and smiles.

"Thanks," he says.

If only I could make the clouds go away forever.

chapter seventeen

I start hanging out at Kate's house a lot. I go over after school once or twice a week. Mom doesn't mind, but she doesn't let me sleep over on school nights anymore, not since I got a D on my last vocabulary quiz. I take the bus home with Kate, and sometimes Jackie drops me back home, and sometimes Mom picks me up. We only live a few miles apart. It's funny to think that Kate's world has always existed so close to mine and we never knew each other until now.

Almost every time I'm over there, Jackie takes us to the mall, and I love it in a way I never thought I would. I love the way it smells like chocolate chip cookies and new shopping bags. I love the shiny life we all lead inside, as if nothing else matters. Jackie always needs to return something or buy something, and she likes to go back and forth several times to get it right. She doesn't work, so it's sort of like her job. And all the trips to the mall give me a chance to spend my forty dollars quickly, before I think about it too hard. I've never had so much fun with money. I buy everything Kate buys, a pink tank top, jelly bracelets with glitter on them, my first lipstick, and a new Tough Love CD. I make sure Mom doesn't see any of it.

Sometimes it's hard to tell who the kid is and who the grown-ups are in Kate's house. Kate's an only child, so it's like her parents are her friends. When I sleep over on the weekend, Greg and Jackie take us out to dinner and the movies and we don't get back until midnight. We eat what we want, watch as much television as we want, go to bed when we want.

Greg couldn't be more different from my dad. Aside from being completely gorgeous, he's also one of the funniest people I've ever met. He's constantly playing these weird jokes on Kate. Once he took all her shoes out of her closet when she wasn't home and replaced them with his own dirty work boots and sneakers. Another time he took a picture of both of us sleeping one night and taped it to the bathroom mirror. When Kate and I saw it the next morning, we almost peed in our pants we were laughing so hard.

On a Sunday after breakfast Kate and I go back up to her room. Kate puts on a jeans skirt and looks me over.

"We're going to church. Want to come?" She says it in this happy way, in a way that doesn't make it sound strange, me going to church with her. "You can wear this." She throws me one of her skirts. It's pink with little green and white embroidered circles on it.

"I don't know," I say, as if she were asking me to go to the moon. Usually I sleep over on Friday nights. This is the first time I've been here on a Sunday morning.

"Why, 'cause you're Jewish?"

"Um, well . . ." But before I can finish, Jackie's in the room.

"Hurry, guys, we're going to be late," she says. "We have to drop off Sonia first."

"Mom, can Sonia come?" Kate says, finishing her lipstick.

"Well . . . ," says Jackie. Something flickers across her eyes. Normally she's excited when I join them in anything. "Aren't you Jewish, hon?"

"Sort of."

"I just don't want you to do anything against your religion."

I feel lost, suddenly. I look at Kate for help, but she's busy fixing her outfit in the mirror.

"I'm not Jewish. Just my mom is. It's not like I'll explode or anything." My words surprise me more than anyone.

Kate turns around and starts laughing. Jackie glares at her, so she puts her hand over her mouth, but doesn't stop.

"Well, you know best. You're always welcome," Jackie says in a stiff way that makes me wonder if she really means "welcome to everything except church." She starts to walk out of the room. "We leave in ten. Quicken the pace, girls."

"Were you joking?" Kate says, still laughing when Jackie leaves the room.

"About what, that I'm going to explode in church?"

"No, that you're not Jewish," Kate says, her eyes beaming, all that sparkling energy focused on me.

I don't really want to answer her. "But what if I do explode?" I whisper, giggling.

"Don't worry," Kate says, laughing harder now. "I'll protect you!" With that she jumps on me like Catwoman and we tumble down on her soft pink rug laughing until we clutch our stomachs in pain. The funniest thing, though, is that I wasn't joking, not one bit. I'm tired of telling people I'm Jewish when I don't really feel Jewish, whatever being Jewish is supposed to feel like.

Kate's church is in a stone building that, I swear, looks like a smaller version of Notre Dame in Paris. Inside are all these stained-glass windows and shiny wooden benches, and the ceiling's a hundred feet up in the air. I don't really listen that carefully to the priest during the sermon, but it sounds like sort of the same stuff the rabbi talks about when we go to temple with my grandparents. I wonder why they're supposed to be so different, being Jewish and being Christian.

They both talk about what God is, and what we can do to be better people, and stories from the Bible that teach us lessons. I like the dark wooden pews, the stone floor, the echoing sounds pinging off the walls. Mostly I love looking at the stained-glass windows, the way the light shows through all the colors like jewels and makes me think of the Taj Mahal. For some reason it makes me happy.

My house is still as heavy as burned bran muffins. It's good that Dad's not sulking around in his bathrobe anymore, but he works such late hours that he's never around. Mom's still working more too. Her classes are all in the morning now, but she spends every night in her office grading papers. We've been getting a lot of takeout pizza these days, something we never used to do.

When Mom's not working, she's asking me how I feel about *everything* with wide, worried eyes. How do you feel about having new friends? How do you feel about Dad working so much? How do you feel about school? I just answer "okay" or "I don't know" most of the time. She likes the "okay" answer better, but "I don't know" is closer to the truth.

Tonight's different, though. I have to get my homework done early because I'm going back to Community. Not for real of course, just to see the sixth-grade play. Sam invited me before our bad conversation. It's almost hard to believe that

Community still exists, that Jack and all my old friends are just having another year as if nothing's changed. It makes my stomach hurt to think about seeing everyone and yet I can't wait to go.

Dad's expected home late because of his new job, so he'll miss the play. I don't really care since I'm not in it. Mom rushes us through a quick dinner of rice and beans. I can barely eat, I have so many thoughts swirling around. The drive there feels different since it's dark out.

When I walk through the big gray front doors, the first thing that hits me is the smell. I didn't even know Community had a smell, but when I walk into the high-ceilinged lobby, with its big jungle-animal mural surrounding me, the combined scent of floor cleaner, and wood, and different foods from people's lunches—hard to describe but so clear to my nose—grabs me like a fast hug.

Mom takes my hand and pulls me and Natasha toward the auditorium. I see Iris, the art teacher, who stands at the front of the auditorium handing out playbills. "Hi, girls!" she shrieks when she sees us. Then she hands me a playbill. The play is called *The Poodle Mystery*. There are all these drawings in the playbill too. I see a picture of a house with a black poodle in the yard and a rainbow above it. It must be Sam's work. We follow Iris toward three seats in the seventh row. As I walk past the rows, I see Connor O'Reilly's father. He waves. He's hard to miss since he's very tall, wears his hair in a ponytail, and has a diamond earring in one ear. He's a dog trainer, kind of a famous one actually, so he must be excited about the play. I see a bunch of other parents who know us too. Each friendly wave makes me sadder and sadder.

"Sonia," I hear a man's deep voice call out behind me. I turn around and see a cheery round face grinning as wide as the open sea.

"Jack!" I say, and run toward him. I dive into his warm arms. I swallow hard so I won't cry. He pulls me back and holds my shoulders.

"Lemme look at you," he says. "Ah, you look even smarter. Your new school must be doing a good job."

My cheeks get hot and I shrug. If I look any smarter it's probably just an accident.

"We miss you," he says, and looks up at Mom.

"Sonia misses you guys too," Mom says, "but she's really doing well at her new school. She joined the cheerleading team." I notice that my mom's voice cracks slightly, like she's trying to hold back tears herself.

"That's great. I'm sure she's dazzling them all."

I'm about to say that I'm not dazzling anyone and Jack will always be the best teacher I've ever had, but the lights flicker, telling everyone to get into their seats.

"That's my signal. Come talk to me after the show," Jack says. He walks off down the aisle toward the back of the stage. I picture everyone rushing around straightening their costumes, bristling with excitement and nervousness. I would give all the green loafers in the world to be back there tonight.

The lights go dim and the stage brightens. A person steps onto the stage in a big fancy dress and a wig piled high with yellow curls. For a second I'm not sure who she is, but then she opens her mouth and Sam's voice travels out into the auditorium. She starts talking about her wonderful family and friends and all her riches. Above all, she has the prettiest poodle anyone has ever seen. Then someone dressed like a poodle comes bounding onstage. Sam leads him through a series of tricks. He sits, lies down, rolls over, and plays dead. Then he does a little Irish jig and the whole audience laughs. Even though his face is covered, I know it must be Connor. Nobody else could be so funny.

The play is great. Basically it's about a family who thinks they're the most perfect people in the world. One day, when no one is home, they leave their safe open by accident. The poodle pulls out a bag filled with jewels and money and buries it in the backyard. Suddenly everyone in the perfect family is blaming one another for the missing riches. At the end, while the family is having a terrible fight, the poodle goes out into the backyard, digs up the bag, and comes in and drops it in the middle of the room. The family just stares and stares in silence. Then the poodle does another jig and the lights go down.

I'm not sure what it all means, but it makes me think

about money and whether my family was happier when it had more. Now that Dad has a new job, if the money thing is true we should all be happy again, right? Not according to the poodle, I guess. Maybe being happy is not how much money you have, but how you spend it.

The audience gives everyone a standing ovation and Sam looks like she's going to burst. I'm close enough to the stage that I can see her hands shaking with excitement. I know I should go backstage and tell her how fantastic she was. I know I should give her a hug and try to melt away the weirdness between us, but all I want to do is leave.

"Let's go see Sam," Mom says, and doesn't wait for my answer. I shuffle behind Natasha as she gallops after Mom.

Sam's parents, Jack, and some of my old classmates from Community surround Sam, who's still in her costume and makeup. Her face is as red as a fire truck. I think she sees me but I'm not sure. I move in closer.

"Sonia!" she finally calls, and waves me over.

"Hi. You were so—" I say, but never get to finish. Everything is a big blur of Mom hugging her, Sadie and Ben hugging me, and Natasha fussing over Sam's costume. Mom gushes over her and I just stand there smiling with jealousy. And just when I think it couldn't get any worse, Connor comes over to Sam and they give each other a huge jumping hug. He's still dressed in most of the poodle costume except for his mask and he looks even more beautiful than I remembered, with his shiny dark hair, green eyes, and long lashes. He and Sam immediately launch into a breakdown of the play, spurting out all the juicy details—I can't believe this and I can't believe that! You were so good! No, *you* were! Did you see when I almost tripped? Did you notice when I forgot my line?

I pull on Mom's sleeve to give her the "let's go" signal. She stops talking to Sadie and looks down.

"I'm really tired," I say. "Can we leave?"

Mom gives me a funny look, but doesn't argue and starts saying her goodbyes. Just before we head off, I touch Sam on the shoulder. "You were so great," I say, trying to sound happy for her, but my voice is low and sad.

"Thanks," she says. Connor finally sees me.

"Hi, Sonia Nadhamuni!" he says.

My stomach does a flip when I hear him say my name so easily. I wave and smile, but I have no words left. Mom puts a hand on my shoulder and I turn toward the door.

"Bye, Sonia," Sam says. I give her a little wave. Then she goes back to talking to the others about the play. The ringing of their happy voices follows me outside into the dark, cold night.

chapter eighteen

After we get home I go straight to my room, climb to the top of my closet, and lie down on the highest shelf. It's a big, wide, sliding-door closet, and I use the row of side shelves as a ladder to get up. I used to hang out here a lot when I was younger. So it's empty except for a pillow and my stuffed bear, who's called Doggie because when I was little I thought all animals were dogs. I would read with a flashlight or just make up stories and whisper them to myself. It's my secret place where I get to just be me. I can hardly fit anymore, but it doesn't matter as I lay my head against the pillow, hold Doggie, and run vocabulary words through my head one by one.

I hear Mom knock on my door. I don't say anything. Then slowly she pushes it open. "Sonia?"

I sit up quickly and bang my head on the ceiling. "Ow."

"Where are you?" Mom asks, now standing in the middle of my dark room.

"In here," I say, and shine my flashlight at her.

"What are you doing?" she says, shielding her eyes from the light.

"I don't know." I start climbing down.

"I didn't think you went up there anymore."

I just shrug and sit on my bed. She turns on my light and sits next to me.

"Jackie called me," she says. I look at her and wonder if they're becoming friends.

"She told me you went to church with them last Sunday and that she heard you telling me on the phone that you were going to brunch, not church."

I open my mouth to tell her we did go to brunch, after church, that I just forgot to tell her about the church part.

"Wait." She holds up her finger. "And Jackie said that you told them you weren't Jewish."

My face burns. I didn't think Jackie was the type of mom to call other moms and tell them this kind of stuff. I put my hands on my cheeks and hang my head. "So I guess you're not going to let me sleep over at Kate's anymore."

Mom lifts my chin up gently to face her.

"I didn't say that, but I do want to know why you lied about going to church, why you said you weren't Jewish."

"Because I was afraid Jackie wouldn't let me come to church with them."

"Really? That's why?"

No, but I wasn't sure how to explain it.

"Do you think Jackie has a problem with you being Jewish?" Mom continues, her voice getting higher, more upset. "Because if that's what's going on, I'm going to have to talk to—"

"No, Mom," I interrupt her. "It's not like that. It's me."

"You never had a problem being Jewish before you met Kate and Jackie."

"It just seemed easier having to explain less. You're not that Jewish either, Mom. You didn't even marry someone Jewish."

Mom's face turns from worried and searching to angry. Her mouth sets in a hard, straight line.

"I may not be the most religious person in the world, but I never would have disrespected my background like that. When I married your dad, I felt as Jewish as I ever did." She wipes the top of her forehead, like she's hot. "Even if other people didn't think so."

I swallow. Why couldn't Jackie have minded her own business?

"I didn't mean to disrespect anything, I just . . ." Mom gets up.

"I don't think it's a good idea to hang out with Kate so much," she says. "You need a break from that household."

And then she's out my door and down the stairs, end of discussion, which is not like Mom at all. But I'm not really surprised. Why would anything go the way I want it to these days?

The sun wakes me up the next day, and it's so bright, it seems to erase all that's come before it. It's our first home game of the season. All the cheerleaders are supposed to wear their uniforms to school like the older girls do. I put mine on and stare in the mirror. I've worn it before, but this is the first time I've worn my uniform to school. The blue and white sweater and skirt fit nicely. I actually look kind of cute and not as silly as Sam might think. I scrape up my hair in a high, bouncy ponytail the way Kate always wears her hair for practice and tie it with a white ribbon. Mom smiles at me when I come downstairs, but then tries to yank down my skirt a little. When I wait for the bus, Cindy and Heather even talk to me, which they hardly ever do. And Mr. Totono gives me a high five when he sees me in the hall.

During English, a folded mint-green note lands on my desk just after Mrs. Langley passes out our corrected vocabulary tests. I got a C, which is better than a D. Mom won't be happy, but I'm too excited to be upset about it. Grades are still strange to me. At Community we never got grades, just written evaluations that explained all the good things we did and the stuff we needed to work on, so I never had to stare at a red C or worse. At Community no one could fail—another thing Alisha thinks is incredible. I unfold the note carefully while keeping a close eye on Mrs. Lonely, as Kate calls her.

Are you going to Peter Hanson's party?
P.S. I'm so psyched for the game!

I stare at it. I haven't been invited to Peter Hanson's party. I look to the left and see Peter sitting in the back. He's busy folding up one of his famous paper airplanes. Two days ago he called me a cow-worshipper under his breath in the cafeteria line. I decided then and there that I hated Peter Hanson.

No, are you? I write back.

She tosses another note my way, this time landing on the floor by my feet. I pretend to scratch my ankle as I pick it up. *Why???* it says. Just then Mrs. Langley shoots me a glance. I quickly tuck the note under my social studies textbook, relieved that I can't reply just yet. I'm not surprised that Peter didn't invite me to his party. Most of the boys on the football team haven't paid much attention to me or, like Peter, have made fun of me. The only boy who has seemed to notice me in a good way is one of Alisha's friends from Bridgeport, Marcus. When I look at him he smiles and then looks away fast. I get the feeling he likes me, but he's never said a word to me, so I don't really know if I'd like him back. This is something I've thought about, though—the only boy who has paid attention to me is black. I wonder if he thinks I'm black.

After school all the cheerleaders stand in a group at the front of the building waiting to walk over to the football field. My legs jitter with nerves. I can't believe that I will actually cheer in front of so many strangers. We huddle together, and most of the girls, led by Jess, are looking around for people to talk about. Jess sticks out her chest in her tight cheerleading sweater and makes jokes about this and that girl, this and that boy. Kate doesn't pay much attention. She's focused and quiet, picking up her legs one at a time to stretch her hamstrings, whispering her cheers into the crisp fall air. I like her even more for ignoring Jess, and I gladly join her stretching while trying to shove the butterflies back down in my stomach. I hope Kate doesn't bring up Peter's party.

This is the time I usually talk to Alisha, except it's been a while because of cheerleading. She sees me and waves. Then she starts walking over in her big T-shirt and baggy jeans.

"Hi, Sonia, guess what?" she says.

"Hey," I say, trying to be all mellow. I bend my leg, bring my ankle up to my butt, and hold it there until I feel my muscles burn.

"I finished my book. And I put in all this stuff about the Taj Mahal. I decided that they fall in love there instead of Paris. Want to read it?" She thrusts her thick black notebook out at me.

"Now?" I'm speaking low to her, almost whispering. I'm not used to talking to Alisha in front of all my cheerleading friends, in front of Kate.

Her face crumples and she pulls back her notebook.

"Not now," she says. "You could take it home."

"Okay" is all I say. I see Kate's eyes dart at me and Alisha. Jess grabs Kate's arm and whispers something in her ear. Alisha holds her notebook out again, waiting. "Can you give it to me tomorrow? I don't want to bring it to the game. It could get stolen." This part is actually true.

"Yeah, sure." Then she takes a deep breath. "So are you ever going to ask your parents if you can come over?" she says, her eyes fierce, hands on hips.

"I'm sorry, I've just been so busy with cheerleading and homework and—"

"I thought you were different," she says, and walks away without another word. I glance back at Kate and Jess. Kate's stretching again and doesn't look at me.

"What's up with her clothes?" Jess says. "She looks like a boy."

I shrug and bend over to touch my toes, staying there as the blood rushes to my head, making me feel a little sick.

The blacktop feels hard yet springy under my feet as we all line up on the track that circles the football field. The players are warming up and mostly parents of the football players are in the bleachers. Jackie's there too, and she winks at me. Jackie says the best time of her life was when she cheered in high school. It makes me sad to think that the best time in her life was when she was a teenager, and I wonder if being a grown-up is any fun at all.

My parents couldn't come because of work, but I'm kind of glad. On one hand, I want to show them how cool our pyramids are, and maybe Mom would think I'm doing something that's actually a real sport, a real performance, just as good as any play. But then again, if my parents were here, my sneakers wouldn't feel so bouncy.

Kate leads us all through some more stretches. Then we practice toe-touches. I've learned how to do a back handspring into a toe-touch. Kate showed me how and now I'm better at it than she is. During the halftime break in the game, we're supposed to do a big cheer in the middle of the field with a pyramid, and then I get to do a cartwheel back handspring, ending with a toe-touch while everyone stays in the pyramid. Whenever I do it in practice everyone watches quietly, like I'm doing something important. And it does feel important, even if it's only a few tricks, even if Sam thinks I'm just running around in a silly outfit.

The game starts and the team goes through all the little

cheers on the sidelines. I see Jess out of the corner of my eye and she's a bit out of step with everyone. It seems like only about five seconds pass before halftime. When we all run out to the field my ankle twists a little, enough to send a shooting pain up my leg.

The cheer goes smoothly and I try to ignore the throbbing. The pyramid isn't a problem because I just stand on the side, but I'm not sure how my ankle is going to handle a cartwheel, back handspring, and toe-touch. I could fall on my face in front of half the school. Kate could think she has it all wrong, that I'm not special, that I'm just a klutzy weird girl.

Kate gets lifted to the top of the pyramid like she's a feather. Everyone's arms and legs are strong and solid. Even the football players pay attention. I clap out the cheer with everyone:

We are strong,
We have the might,
Go blue and yellow,
Fight, fight, fight!

On the last "fight" I run. In a flash I decide not to care about my ankle, or Kate, or Peter Hanson's party, or my sad dad, or my nervous mom, or Sam, or taking the money from Mom, or the D I got on my vocabulary test, or whether I want to be Jewish or not. All I care about is the way I feel when my feet hit the ground after the back handspring. The way I pop up into the air, my legs so high they practically make a V. The satisfying sting in my palms after smacking my toes harder than I ever have. It's a toe-touch for the ages.

Everyone, even Peter Hanson, starts clapping and *whoo-hoo*ing as the whole team runs back to the sidelines. Kate pats me on the back, and to my amazement so do Jess and a few other girls. I can't feel my ankle anymore. It's completely numb. I can only feel the smile that stretches across my face so wide, it hurts. Wonder what Mom would think about cheerleading now.

chapter nineteen

The envelope says *Sonia Nadamoony*. I hold the card in my hand, closing and opening it again to make sure it's real. There are balloons on the front with the word "party" in gold letters. Inside it says:

A Birthday Party for Peter!
WHEN: Saturday, November 15, 3 p.m.
WHERE: 125 Birch Street
RSVP: Margaret Hanson, 555-4658

I receive this invitation four days after the game. I had finally told Kate that I wasn't invited to Peter's party, since she asked me again why I wasn't going. She said Peter probably just didn't know my last name, because the rest of the cheerleading team had been invited. I know this can't be true unless Peter is secretly deaf: Mrs. Langley calls attendance using both first and last names every morning. Kate said she was going to say something to Peter. I said, "No, don't," but meant "Please do," even though I don't like Peter. Kate somehow knew I really wanted her to say something and now I'm holding this invitation. Maybe my ESP powers have transferred from Sam to Kate.

"Can I go?" I ask Mom. Natasha and I are sharing a bowl of popcorn while Mom is cooking lentil stew. Dad's working late again and won't be home for dinner. And he's leaving for Hong Kong in a week to visit some factory where they actually print the books. This makes Mom stir the lentil stew too fast. Natasha throws a piece of popcorn at me and it bounces off my forehead. I have to throw one back at her, which means she has to throw one back at me. Before I know it, there's more popcorn on the floor than in the bowl.

"When is it, again?" Mom calls from the stove.

"Next Saturday, I told you," I say, ducking. A piece of popcorn flies over my head.

"Who is this boy? You never talk about him."

I take a piece of popcorn, throw it into the air, try to catch it in my mouth, and miss. Mom turns around and sees the popcorn-covered floor.

"Come on, girls," she says with tired eyes and tight lips. I get down on my knees fast and start to pick it up. Natasha follows.

"Sorry," I say. I hope I haven't just blown my chances of going to the party. "He's a boy in my class. He also plays on the football team. The whole cheerleading team is going." I don't tell her the me-not-being-invited, being-invited story.

"A cheerleader going to a football player's party. It sounds like high school. When did you get so old?" Mom looks at me. Her eyes are softer now. "You can go. I just want to talk to his parents," she says, stirring some more.

She can't do that. That's what parents do for little kids. Didn't Mom just notice how things were different, how I was older now? I think about Sam and our sleepovers, the Magic 8 Ball, ESP, and camping trips. It suddenly seems so young, so *nursery school*.

"Do you have to?" I say, and then wish I could take back the whine in my voice. Mom hates whining.

"I don't know these people. You'll understand when you're a mother."

Who knows if I'll even be a mother? All I know is that I'll bet a thousand dollars Jackie isn't calling Peter's parents. But I'll take what I can get. Mom and I haven't talked about the Jewish thing since. We just look at each other funny and talk about stuff that we have to talk about like how much homework I have, when I need a ride to what, and what I want for dinner. When she asked me how the game went, I said, "Pretty good," and that was it.

I go up to my room and look through my closet for

something to wear to the party. I start grabbing skirts and shirts off their hangers and hold them up in my mirror. Wrong. All my clothes are wrong. Then I see it, way back in the closet under a plastic dry-cleaning bag—my red velvet dress, the one Dad brought back from a trip to London last year. It's the only present he's ever bought me without Mom's help. I've worn it only once, to my mom's cousin's wedding. It's fitted on top, with satin trimming on the scoop neck and the edges of the sleeves. The pleated skirt is what my mom calls tea-length, which means it goes all the way down to my ankles but not to the floor. I put it on. It still fits, and it makes me feel like the Indian princess I was named after.

On Thursday, a little over a week before the party, Kate and I walk to the late buses after practice. It's a beautiful day, not too cold, but crisp and sunny. The leaves have started to fall, leaving big, bright open spots showing through the trees. I blink, wondering when this all happened, all these changes. How did I not notice?

"Do you want to do something tonight?" Kate asks.

"Sure," I say, even though I know Mom won't let me.

"How come we never go over to your house?"

I look at her, the late-fall sun making her hair look orange, making her blue eyes even brighter.

"No reason." Ha, right. Natasha would probably play her

drums the whole time or just be annoying. Mom would be weird and serious and ask Kate too many questions. There would be no Pringles, no mall, no reality TV. And Dad, well, who knows what Dad will be like on any given day? I thought getting a new job would make him feel better, and sometimes he does seem more like himself. Sometimes he doesn't. Kate would probably want to go right back to her house the minute she stepped in mine.

"Can I? I'm sick of my house," she says.

"Uh, sure," I say.

Kate takes out her new sparkly pink cell phone and calls Jackie and asks her to pick her up after dinner. When she's done she hands it to me.

"Wanna call your mom?"

I take the phone and stare at the rhinestones on the cover. It's like my hands are frozen. They literally won't move.

"What's wrong?" Kate says.

"Nothing," I say, and snap the phone shut. "You know what, I'm sure it's fine."

"Okay," Kate says. "If you're sure."

chapter twenty

When we finally arrive, my heart pounds as we head in through the garage door, which no one ever locks.

I walk in down the few stairs leading into the kitchen, Kate following me, and look around. No Mom.

"Wow," she says. "Your house is so cool. It's like totally modern and totally old at the same time."

"Thanks," I say, not really knowing what she means.

She dumps her backpack on the floor and goes to examine the collection of Buddhas on the shelves behind the kitchen table.

"Sonia," Mom calls from the hallway. I freeze. She rounds the corner, Natasha trailing behind her holding her drumsticks. Natasha sees us and stops walking.

"Hi, Kate," Mom says. "I didn't know you were coming over." She smiles at her with her mouth, but not her eyes.

"Sonia said it would be okay," Kate says in her bubbly way. "Is that your sister?" Kate points to Natasha, who's hiding by the stairs chewing on a piece of her hair.

"Yup," I say.

"Natasha," Mom says. "Come say hi."

"Hey," Kate says. "Are those drumsticks?" Natasha comes closer and holds them forward, nodding.

"You play the drums?"

Natasha nods.

"That is so awesome! Will you play something for me?" Kate asks, her smile wide, eyes bright.

Natasha glows and nods furiously.

Then Kate turns to Mom. "Mrs. Nadhamuni," she says perfectly, "that's a really pretty necklace." She steps forward to see it better. Mom fingers the fancy silver circle that hangs from a chain she got from India years ago. She wears it so much, I don't even notice it anymore.

"Oh, thanks." Mom touches it as if trying to remember it herself.

Mom turns to me and clears her throat. "Sonia, can I talk to you for a sec?" She doesn't wait for an answer, just starts walking to her bedroom. I look at Kate to tell her I'll be right back, but she's busy looking at the tapestry that hangs over the fireplace in the den area. Our first floor is really one big room, kitchen, den, and living room all blending into one. There's nowhere to hide.

I follow Mom into the bedroom and sit down on the big lumpy bed. Mom closes the door and faces me. Her room smells like old coffee. I see two mugs on the dresser.

"What's going on?" Mom says, hands on hips. "First of all, it's a school night. You didn't ask her to sleep over, did you?"

"No, but I don't have any homework anyway," I say.

"Just tell me why you didn't ask me first."

"Because you said you didn't want me to see her anymore, but she asked if she could come over. What was I supposed to say? No?"

"Yes, you were. And I didn't say I didn't want you to see her anymore, just that you needed a break," she says.

"Do I have to tell her to go home?" I say. My mouth is dry. I try to imagine telling Kate she can't stay.

Mom lets out a big sigh, lifts up her glasses, rubs her eyes.

"No, I guess not," she says, and opens the door. "Look, I have some work to do. Just let Natasha play with you guys, and we're going to talk about this later."

"Oh, come on!" I say without thinking. "She'll just be a dork." I'm sure Kate didn't plan on babysitting a six-year-old.

"Sonia, you're really pushing it" is all Mom says before she opens the door, motioning to me to go first.

When I come back to the front of the house, I don't see Kate or Natasha; then I hear talking and laughing upstairs.

Kate's sitting on the floor with Natasha, painting my sister's nails purple.

"Hey, little squirmer. Hold still," she says. Natasha wiggles her other hand at me. "I had some in my bag," Kate says. "It must be so much fun to have a little sister."

Natasha blinks at me and goes back to gazing at Kate while she paints each nail carefully.

I don't answer. I sit down on the bottom of Natasha's red bunk bed.

Then Kate asks Natasha to play something. Natasha blows on her little fingers a few seconds and gets her sticks. She plays a couple different beats that I've heard ten thousand times, and finishes off with a stupid and very loud solo. Kate claps her hands wildly after she's done.

"Wow, you should totally start a girl band," Kate says.

"A what?" Natasha says. "Oh, no. I chipped one!" she cries, examining her nails.

"She's only six," I say, and sigh.

"I'll fix it," Kate says, rushing to her side with the bottle of nail polish. I'm starting to feel like Natasha and Kate are babysitting me. Everyone likes Natasha. She's funny and cute and little. It's always that way. As soon as she was born, people started ignoring me at family holidays, everyone fussing over baby Natasha. I'm always the serious one, the one reading in the corner who people leave alone. Sometimes I like it that way. Sometimes I don't.

After Natasha's manicure and performance and second manicure, we all go into my room.

"I can't believe this is your room," Kate says.

"How come?" I look at the blue and green tie-dyed comforter. The beige rug, the huge overflowing bookshelf, my enormous dark wooden desk. I wonder if I have anything weird on it, like the travel section of the newspaper or some embarrassing thing I was writing.

"It looks like a room for someone much older," she says, "like your parents or something." My cheeks start to burn. She sits at my desk and leans back in the big leather chair. Natasha sits cross-legged on the floor, still checking out her nails. Kate takes a pen out of the red leather pen holder and starts doodling something on a yellow lined pad I got from Dad. "I know!" she says, and holds up her drawing. "We could give it a makeover."

"A makeover?"

"Your room." She shows me her drawing. It's a fat, bubbly diagram of my room. Right now all the furniture is flat against the wall. But Kate's drawing has the bookshelf on a catty-corner, and the bed and desk switched, so that the bed would be under the other windows and the desk would be in the center.

"And we could tie your curtains with ribbons and maybe add a few more pillows on your bed. It would look soooo good."

"Yeah!" Natasha says, throwing herself belly-first on my bed.

"I don't know," I say.

"You'll love it," Kate says, and gets up. She puts her hands on one side of my desk. "Help me move this?"

So we get to work, moving furniture, rearranging, organizing. I wonder why Kate cares so much. I would never suggest that Kate change her room around. But then again, it's perfect. We move what we can into the middle of the room, taking stuff off the desk and books out of the bookshelves. Then Kate picks up a pillow and whacks me with it. I whack her back and she falls on her butt laughing. Then Natasha whacks me, making me fall, and suddenly we're a big snowball of pillows and arms and legs.

Mom comes running up the stairs and bursts through my doorway.

"What on earth is going on?" Mom says. We freeze.

Kate jumps up, smooths her hair, and wipes some sweat off her forehead.

"We're giving Sonia's room a makeover! Don't worry, Mrs. Nadhamuni, it will look great. Do you have any blue or white ribbon?"

"I don't know if this is such a good idea," Mom says.

I look at the sour, worried expression on Mom's face, as if we're painting the walls black rather than basically cleaning up my room in a way it's never been cleaned before, and I wish I could take a big whack at her with a pillow. She starts walking around picking up a couple of books and putting them down. I wonder if I had that same worried expression on my face when Kate asked me at first.

"Mom, it'll take just as much time to put it back the way it was. Can we just finish it?" I say. I have to admit it's been fun, kind of like when Mary Poppins comes in and cleans up the nursery.

Mom runs her fingers through her frizzy hair. I bet Kate could give her some good style tips.

"Just get it in some kind of order before dinner," she says. Then she heaves a big sigh, which she does a lot these days, and walks out.

We all start giggling and then Kate stands up and asks me to take one side of the desk. We push it under the big windows where my bed used to be. We put the bed in the corner under the smaller window and it looks much cozier. I go to the linen closet and get more pillows with white covers, which Kate fluffs and arranges on the bed. We find blue ribbon in Mom's gift-wrapping stash, and Kate ties the plain white curtains in a special way so that they bubble out. We put the bookshelf on a diagonal and reshelve all the books neatly. We clean up all the papers and clothes and books on the floor. Kate throws a sheet over my desk chair and ties more blue ribbon around the back of it, so it looks fancy. We even get some of Natasha's blue paint and Kate paints big fat flowers on the front of the dresser around the knobs. When we're done we all collapse on the floor in exhaustion.

"I can't believe you did this." I turn my face to Kate. "It's like magic."

"No it's not," Kate says. "My mom rearranges stuff all the time. It's easy."

"Dinner!" Mom calls. My stomach flips at hearing the word. I hadn't even thought about what Mom would make and I pray it's not eggplant-tofu casserole.

"Mrs. Nadhamuni, come check it out!" Kate calls down the stairs as if she's talking to her own mother. She always acts like she knows someone well even when she doesn't. Jackie does that too.

Mom walks in slowly and puts her hand over her mouth. I see her eyes travel over the bed, the curtains, the flowers on the dresser.

"Oh, my God," she says in a way that's so deep and serious, it sends a chill through me. What if she yells at Kate, makes her go home?

"Mom, we can put it back, don't freak out."

"Put it back? It's amazing! Kate, I think you have a lucrative career in interior design waiting for you."

Kate does her jumping, clapping thing, and hugs me and Natasha. Now we're all jumping up and down and hugging.

"You guys must be hungry after all that work. Wash your hands and come on down," Mom says like she's on a game show. Now she's smiling with her mouth and her eyes.

chapter twenty-one

My nose twitches at the smells from the kitchen. It's definitely not eggplant, but I can't really tell yet. It smells sort of, well, brown. I finally see the table. There it is, in the middle. A big, brown, non-meat meat loaf. Next to it is a salad, a platter of roasted cauliflower, and a bowl of brown rice. Kate's just smiling, looking around, still pink in her cheeks from our redecorating work. She has no idea what's about to happen to her.

We sit down, me next to Kate, Natasha and Mom across from us. The chair at one head of the table where Dad usually sits is empty. Kate immediately puts her napkin on her lap, so I do too, even though I normally don't. I see Mom does as well and nudges Natasha to do the same.

"Is Dad coming home for dinner?" I ask, but I kind of hope he's not. It's easier when he's not around. Before she can answer, I hear the garage door open. Dad walks in holding his briefcase, his head down, his eyes dark.

Mom gets up quickly and walks over to him. He looks up like she just woke him. She says something softly and he lifts his weary eyes our way.

"Hi, Daddy," Natasha yells, and runs over for a hug.

"Hi, Mr. Nadhamuni. It's so great to finally meet you," Kate says loudly, and gives him a big wave. Dad squints at her as if he's staring into bright light and can't help but smile. I want to hug Kate right now for her Mary Poppins ways. You just can't not be happy around her.

Dad takes off his coat and sits down. A thick silence moves over the table like fog. I give a sideways glance to Kate, who has her hands clasped, resting on the table, and then I remember. She's waiting for us to say grace. Her family always does, even at a restaurant. We never say grace. I didn't even know what saying grace was all about until I started going over to Kate's. It's nice, saying thanks for all that food, except when it's tofu-eggplant casserole. Mom asks for our plates and spoons everything onto them. I hold my breath and watch Kate, who still has her hands clasped.

"I hope this isn't rude," she says. "But I was just wondering. Do Jewish people and, um, Indian people say grace?" I cough a little.

Dad drags his fingers through his hair and looks at Mom.

She turns back to Kate. "Well, I think historically Jews have said grace after a meal," Mom says, and pauses.

"But if you go way back and look at different religions, like Hinduism for example . . . ," Dad pipes up before taking a pause too.

"I think what we mean is . . ." Mom laughs a little. "The truth is we don't really know. We can say grace if you'd like."

"Oh, no, it's nice to get a break," Kate says with another one of her beaming smiles. We start eating. I watch Kate as she pokes the non–meat loaf and decides to eat a piece of cauliflower instead. She chews slowly and then faster.

"This is really good. What is it?" she asks.

She must be lying, but she's being polite. I taste some too. At least Mom put butter and salt on it.

"Cauliflower," Mom says.

"I've never eaten cauliflower."

"You've never eaten cauliflower?" my entire family says at exactly the same time. Everybody stops chewing and we all crack up. During the rest of dinner Kate tells lots of funny stories about how bad Jackie's cooking is, and how once a turkey exploded in the oven on Thanksgiving, which explains why they go out so much. We joke and laugh like Kate comes over all the time, like that's the way my family is. I don't think Kate liked the non–meat loaf much, but she did eat a lot of cauliflower. It's the best dinner we've had in a long time.

When we're back in my room waiting for Jackie to come,

Kate fusses with the pillows one more time, then sits down on my bed cross-legged. I sit at my newly prettified desk and lean back in the chair.

"Your family's so nice," she says.

"Thanks." I spin around in the chair to face her. At least tonight they were.

"Like a real family," she says, looking nervous.

I stare at her. "What do you mean? Your family's awesome."

"But you have a sister to hang with, a mom who can cook, a dad."

"What are you talking about? Your dad's way cooler than mine."

"Yeah, no, I mean, a dad who wears a suit and everything and who is so normal, I guess. When you said he was Indian, I just expected something different," she says, her eyes cast down at the rug.

"What did you expect?" I ask.

"Um," she says, looking even more nervous. "More foreign, I guess."

"Like with an accent and turban on his head," I say.

"No, that's not what I mean. Don't listen to me. I don't know what I'm talking about. You look just like him, by the way." She looks away and starts checking out my closet. "What are you going to wear to Peter's party?"

"I'm not sure," I say, happy to change the subject, but I

can't help but wonder how Kate would feel about my dad if he did wear a turban and have an accent.

"Let's find you an outfit!" Kate says. I don't tell her about my red dress in the back of my closet. I want to surprise her. She looks through the few skirts and dresses I have and pairs them with different shirts, holding them up on me. Neither of us gets excited about anything.

"You'll just come over and borrow something," she says.

"Yeah," I say, and though I'm sure she'd have something really cute for me to wear, nothing will look better than the red dress.

"Hey, Kate," I say as she tosses a tight white shirt that I hate back into my closet, "my dad isn't that normal, you know."

She whips around, searching my eyes. "What do you mean?"

I want to tell her how strange things have been with my family, how Dad was out of work, how he found a new job, but that he still seems depressed. I worry that she'll tell Jess. Worse, what if she doesn't seem to care or doesn't understand? "My dad can be so serious" is all I say. "Greg is so funny."

"He is, but he's always joking. I mean *always*. I can never talk to him about serious stuff."

"Well, sometimes I wish my dad was funnier."

"I know! Let's swap. Every other weekend we'll trade dads," she says, her eyes bright and flashing.

"Deal."

✦ ✦ ✦

The next morning, Kate and I get off our busses at the same time and walk into school together. I see Alisha, who's sitting on the front steps. I give her a small smile, but Alisha keeps her eyes straight down.

"Aren't you friends with her?" Kate asks when we pass her.

"Not lately," I say, shrugging, because right now I don't care.

chapter twenty-two

A week later, Jackie beeps the horn in the driveway and Mom walks out with me and waves to her. She kisses me on the forehead, tells me I look gorgeous, and goes back inside. Mom seems much more relaxed about Kate since she came over.

I get in the car. Jackie has the music turned up. She listens to all the new rock bands and knows more about the latest hits than Kate does.

"Hey," Kate says as I settle in next to her. My skirt billows up as I sit down, like I'm sitting in the middle of a red rose. I finger the satin edging on the end of my sleeve. Mom even French-braided my hair.

"Wow!" Jackie says, turning around. "You look like a princess."

My heart leaps and I blush. "Thanks."

Then she looks at Kate. "Hon, was the party supposed to be so dressy? Maybe we should have gotten you something nicer?" I look at Kate, who's staring at me in more of a surprised way than a wow-you-look-great way. She's wearing a short aqua-blue dress with a short black cardigan over it and black shoes with no backs, her hair down and wavy. She looks the way teen movie stars do.

"You look so pretty," I say in a small voice.

"Thanks." She opens her little black beaded purse. "You too," she says with her eyes down as she searches for something in her purse. She takes out a compact mirror and checks her lipstick. Other than Jackie asking a few questions, Kate and I barely talk the whole car ride.

Peter's house is on the other side of Maplewood, where the really big houses are. All the houses are actually pretty big in this town, so the really big ones are kind of like mansions. Jackie drives down a long bumpy driveway. At the end is a huge white house with black shutters and an enormous front porch. Acres of land surround the house. I even see horse stables in the distance.

"Now, this is a house," Jackie says as we get out. "Let me know how the rich live," she calls before speeding away.

Mrs. Hanson opens the door. She smiles a squinty smile and touches her poufy blondish-grayish hair. She says we both look fabulous and takes our gifts. At least I followed Kate's advice and bought Peter a Tough Love CD.

Mrs. Hanson leads us through a massive living room and down some back stairs to the basement. I think of our basement with its lumpy couches and water-stained carpet, and the exercise bike sitting in the corner. *This* basement is a kid's paradise. My feet sink into the thick carpet. A huge sectional couch sits in the middle like an island. Two real pinball machines and the biggest flat-screen television I've ever seen stand against the wall. On one side of the room sits a table with a long submarine sandwich cut up into a million pieces on it. There are also bowls of pickles, chips, and M&M's, and a full setup of sodas and juices. My mouth waters at the thought of eating cold cuts and potato chips and drinking bright orange soda.

Kate pushes past me and runs up to Jess. Peter is standing in the corner with a few other boys. One of them punches Peter in the arm and he punches back. Then the boys gawk at Kate for a few seconds.

"Hi, Kate," Peter finally says. She waves to them and they start a new round of arm punching. Jess and Kate give each other a look, but I don't know if it's about me or Peter. I see Ann, the other alternate, and quickly grab a place by her side.

"Hi," she says. "That's a really pretty dress." She seems like she means it.

"Thanks," I say, and hope Kate can hear her. "Yours is

too." Though she's not wearing a dress. She has on a pink button-down shirt and a short khaki skirt. None of the other girls are nearly as dressed up as I am. They're all either wearing little sweaters and dresses like Kate or shirts and skirts like Ann. Kate huddles with Jess, who's also in a sweater and dress, but hers is pink and white and much tighter than Kate's. They whisper something while shooting glances at Peter and his friends on the other side of the room. I wonder why no one is eating. I wonder why the boys and girls are on separate sides of the room.

Peter's mother comes down with a platter of potato salad and sees the untouched food. "You're all growing children. Eat!" she says, and starts handing out paper plates.

I take one, relieved that someone is going to make us eat. Everyone gets food, but as soon as Mrs. Hanson leaves, the groups split up again, girls around the couch, boys near the pinball machines. I sit quietly next to Ann, secretly loving the sub stuffed with ham, salami, and turkey. I also piled my plate high with potato chips and M&M's. I see that I've taken more than any other girl. Kate's picking at a scoop of potato salad and Jess is doing the same.

"Where'd you get that dress, Sonia?" Jess calls to me. My heart speeds up.

"London," I say, hoping this isn't what she expects.

"You look like you should be in *The Nutcracker*."

A couple of the other girls giggle. Even Kate. I figure

there are worse insults than looking like I'm part of a famous ballet.

"Thanks," I say again, all bright and happy, knowing this will confuse her. More giggles. I smooth my skirt. The touch of velvet comforts me and I remember why I love the dress. Who cares if it's different from what everyone else is wearing? It's the best present I ever got. I look at Kate but she doesn't meet my eye.

After the conversation turns away from my dress and back to the boys, Peter puts an empty bottle of Sprite on the coffee table. He lays it on its side and there's a hush in the room.

"Spin the Bottle," Jess whispers to Kate.

People start forming a circle around the table. I sit down on the floor next to Ann, who starts biting her lip. Kate and Jess sit together on the other side of the circle and continue to whisper and shoot quick glances at the boys. I cross my legs and pull my skirt over them. It's full enough to completely cover me, feet included, and it feels safe under there.

Peter runs up the stairs for a minute and comes back down.

"She's out in the garden," he says, meaning his mother. "She'll be out there forever."

No one says anything and everyone stares at the bottle. Then Jess jumps up and pulls her cardigan tight across her body.

"I'll spin first," she says. Her eyes are bright and big. She whips the bottle around and it points to me. "Do-over," she says. "We all have to be mixed together. You guys"—she points to a few of the boys next to Peter—"sit on this side."

There's a fit of sneaky laughs, but they do as she says and sit themselves in between the girls. A quiet boy named Danny, with blond curls hanging over his eyes, sits between me and Ann. He scrunches up his knees and plays with his sneaker laces as if they're the most exciting things in the world.

Jess spins again and it points to a boy named Jeff, the shortest boy at the party. Another round of choky laughs ripples through the room. Jess walks over to where Jeff's sitting, kneels down, puts her hands on his shoulders, and kisses him hard on the mouth. She makes twisty motions with her head like they do in the movies. Suddenly my body feels cold, like I jumped in ice water.

Jeff, his face still red from Jess's kiss, gets up and spins. It points to Ann. He walks over to her and gives her a quick kiss on the mouth. She keeps her eyes open and her arms at her sides like a soldier. Then she spins and gets Peter. He flashes his green eyes at her and smiles. She kisses him so quickly, I wonder if she even touched his lips.

Then Peter spins and gets Kate. I catch my breath for her even though she's been a jerk this whole party, because I know she's dying of happiness inside. She doesn't smile, she just stares at him and waits. He smiles a sneaky half smile, comes over, and kneels down in front of her. She closes her eyes and they kiss carefully, not too hard, not too fast. When she opens her eyes again they look at each other all intense, until Danny and a couple of other boys start *whoo-hoo*ing. Kate goes all red and turns to Jess, whose eyes are as big as saucers. They share some silent secret, and it makes me think of Sam with a pang in my heart.

"This is boring," Jess yells out. "Let's play Two Minutes in the Closet."

Kate shoots Jess a look of surprise. Now that I know what Spin the Bottle is, I can figure out the next game—more of the same, only longer. Kate gets Danny. They go off into the big walk-in closet in the corner of the room. Jess, of course, is timing them. When they come out Kate looks mad. Did he kiss too much or not enough, I wonder? Danny keeps his eyes hidden under his curls.

He spins. I watch the bottle, the swirl of translucent green, as it slows and stops. In. Front. Of. Me. I didn't actually believe someone would get me. I didn't actually believe that I'd have to be locked in an actual closet with an actual boy.

Danny doesn't look at me, he just goes back into the closet. I know Kate's eyes are on me, but I won't meet hers, not for all the money in the world. I stand up, smooth my skirt, and follow him. I feel a little dizzy and wonder if fainting would be easier than going into that closet.

I've practiced some kisses in the mirror by myself and on a Tough Love poster that Sam has hanging on her bedroom wall. We both practiced. I always kissed the guy with the longest hair, she the shortest. But posters and mirrors don't kiss back.

The closet is bigger than I thought, with only a few coats hanging and stacks of board games on the top shelves. It smells like newly cut wood. The light goes off automatically when the doors close, but somehow Danny knows where the switch is and clicks it on again. He brushes away a curl and smiles.

"Your friend Kate is a prude," he says.

"Is she?" I say, knowing full well that if he'd said that before this party, I would have stood up for her.

"Are you black?" Danny asks, but in a telling voice, not an asking voice.

"No," I say, and swallow hard, not sure anymore if that's the right answer.

"So what are you?"

"A girl," I say.

"Aren't you an Indian?" he asks.

I get that fainty feeling again and Danny's pretty-boy face starts to change into something ugly, really ugly.

"I don't want to kiss you," I say.

"Just like your friend Kate. Too bad," he says, then he puts his hands on my shoulders, presses his mouth against mine, and sticks his tongue in. He tastes salty, like potato chips. His fingers dig into my shoulders as he holds me in place. I close my eyes and keep my hands by my sides and wonder if everyone's first kiss is like this. There's a rap on the door. The two minutes are up. He stops kissing me, shakes his curls back over his eyes, and opens the door. I quickly wipe my mouth and know that even if my face is red, my dress will be redder.

Everyone stares as I sit down. I look around waiting for Danny to spin again, and realize with a catch in my throat that it's my turn. I grab the Sprite bottle. I want to spin so hard it just might dissolve into thin air. Then Peter runs up and takes the bottle from me.

"I hear my mom coming. Spread out," he commands in a harsh whisper. And everyone does except me. I just sit there staring at where the bottle once was.

"You kids ready for cake?" Mrs. Hanson says as she enters the room smiling and blinking, still holding her gardening scissors. My body relaxes like a balloon leaking air as I wait for cake.

Mom is late coming to pick us up, me and Kate, and we both have to watch everyone leave. Even Peter leaves with his dad and his older brother to go sailing or hiking or something, I don't exactly hear. Mrs. Hanson asks if we want to wait inside, but before we can answer, she says it's a beautiful day and leads us to the front porch with glasses of lemonade as if it's the dead of summer. It's really a gray sort of day, with a breeze that's almost freezing but not quite.

We sit on a white wooden bench facing the large circular driveway.

"Why are you being such a jerk to me?" I say, the blood pulsing in my temples. A squirrel darts across the blacktop, stops for a second, eyeing us, and continues toward the woods.

"Really? Have I been?" Kate asks, playing with the silver cross on her necklace.

"Yes, you have," I say, and suddenly feel limp, like I've been walking all day in the sun.

"I'm sorry," she says.

"Did I do something wrong?"

"No," she says, and then smiles all goofy.

"What?" I say.

"Here's the truth. I was embarrassed by your dress. It's just so fancy. I'm totally sorry. You could have borrowed something."

Her voice trails off and her eyes fill with tears. I watch her fingers twist the silver cross around and around.

I look away. If I look at her any longer, watch her crying, I'll tell her it's okay, and it's not. I thought she liked me because I was different, but maybe she just liked me because she thought she could make me the same.

Mom finally pulls up. She's staring straight ahead, not smiling, not waving, not doing the things she normally does. We hop off the bench and climb into the car.

"How was the party?" Mom asks in a quiet, faraway voice.

"Really fun," Kate says.

No one speaks another word until we get to Kate's house.

"Call me later," she says, getting out of the car, and I nod, knowing I won't call her anytime soon.

I start crying in the backseat on the way home, just like that. The tears fall out and my body shakes, but it feels good. I've wanted to cry like this for a long time. It takes Mom a minute to even notice. When she does, she pulls over.

"What? What's wrong?" She spins around and looks at me, panicked.

Her reaction is not like Mom at all, but nothing's the way it's supposed to be anymore, so I don't think much of it. Normally, though, when I cry Mom seems to know exactly why without me having to explain. She's always so calm about it. She just rubs my back and waits until I'm ready to talk.

"It's just . . ." I try to think of the thing that's making me cry right now. Is it that Kate became a totally different person because of one wrong red dress? Is it the way I can still feel Danny's hard skinny fingers pressing down on my shoulders? Is it the way I can still hear his questions echoing inside me?

"It's . . . everything," I say between sobs.

Mom gets out of the front seat and comes in back next to me. I bury my face in her shoulder and she hugs me tight.

"I'm not sure I want to be Kate's friend anymore," I say, wiping my face.

"How come?" Mom asks.

"She said she was embarrassed by my dress."

Mom puts her hands on my shoulders and looks me over. "Why? You look gorgeous."

"It wasn't the right style. Too fancy," I manage.

"Well, maybe to Kate, but that's for you to answer for yourself."

"And a boy kissed me at the party," I say. I wonder if this will make her angry. I straighten up, wipe my nose, but keep my eyes down.

"Did you want him to kiss you?" she asks, pronouncing every word carefully.

"No, not really. We were all playing a game, Spin the Bottle."

"Oh," she says. She takes a few seconds before continuing. "So you felt like you had to let him kiss you?"

"Yes," I say, lifting my eyes.

"You don't ever have to kiss anyone unless you want to. Even if it's embarrassing not to. I think being embarrassed is easier to get over than kissing boys you don't want to kiss."

"I guess," I say, and know that she's right. It would be nice to feel so free, to do whatever I felt was right and true. And then I remember that I used to feel that way all the time.

"It's hard, though, in a game like that, with everyone watching. I know, I played it, although I was a little older than you are now," she says, and smooths my hair off my forehead. "You didn't do anything wrong." I take an easy, slow breath. That's all I wanted her to say.

"Mom, I'm sorry I said I wasn't Jewish."

She just stares at me for a moment. It scares me. "And there as well, you didn't do anything wrong," she finally says. "I did. You should be able to ask questions and try things, and you should be able to talk to me about anything. But Sonia . . ." She says my name again, serious and slow. Her voice is too deep. Now I notice her eyes are red, like she's been crying too.

"Something's happened, and I know you're already upset, but I have to tell you," she goes on. She puts her warm hands on my shoulders. I can hear a soft *thud, thud* in my ears.

"It's your dad," she says, and then I can't hear any more. There's too much in my brain. Like an overloaded computer, I come crashing to a stop.

chapter twenty-three

My father's gone. Well, not gone—he's disappeared. Dad was supposed to show up in Hong Kong last night, but when he wasn't at some big meeting this morning, they called his office. His office called the airport and found out that he never boarded the plane, which is actually a good thing, Mom says. It means that wherever he is, he's not all the way in Hong Kong.

I think of how Dad used to play hide-and-seek with me and Natasha. He picked the best hiding places, under the sink in the laundry room, or in the little closet I always forgot was in the guest room. He'd have to call out sometimes to give us hints. I'm tempted to go looking for him now, in the closets, in the laundry room. He must be close by, just playing a game.

But this is not a game. The police are here, and Mom's

showing them pictures of Dad. Natasha and I are supposed to be watching TV upstairs, but instead we're sitting on the stairs listening to every word.

"When was the last time you spoke with your husband?" the policeman asks.

Mom is quiet for a moment. "Two days ago. When he left."

"Did he say anything out of character?"

"No," she says. "He seemed excited for the trip."

"Had anything unusual been going on before he left?"

Silence again.

"Actually, yes," Mom finally says. She continues in a low voice, the kind of hush-hush voice she uses with Dad when she needs to talk about things Natasha and I aren't supposed to hear. We both creep down to a lower stair.

"He, my husband . . ." She clears her throat before going on. "He's been suffering from a clinical depression ever since he lost his previous job about six months ago."

"Was he taking any medication for it?" the policeman asks.

"Yes," she says, and mentions the pills Dad was taking. "But he wasn't getting better, or at least, not as fast as he did the last time, twelve years ago."

"Has he ever disappeared before or . . ." The policeman pauses and coughs a little before going on. "Attempted to take his own life?"

"No, never." On the word "never," her voice cracks. I can hear a few muffled sobs, and the sound of Mom blowing her nose and the policeman saying that he's sorry, and that he'll do everything he can to help find Dad.

Natasha's sucking her thumb, something she hasn't done in ages. I brush her hand away from her mouth. "Is Dad coming back?" she says, and puts her thumb right where it was before.

"Of course," I say, knowing that's what Mom would want me to say, and I wish I believed it. That night I can't sleep and I can't stop crying. I don't care anymore about what happened at Peter's party. It's small and stupid now. I just want my father back.

Eventually I stop crying and go to my closet. I take out my red dress, slip it on over my nightgown, and get back into bed. I pretend that the dress is made out of the sari silk I saw drying in the fields on the way to the Taj Mahal. I pull it tight around me, wishing I really were an Indian princess and could use my magical princess powers to make anything happen, make my father come back with a flick of my fingers. Maybe, I think as I drift off to sleep, Dad went to India instead. Maybe he missed the mango trees.

On Monday Mom keeps Natasha and me out of school and calls in sick herself. She's on and off the phone a lot. Talking to my grandparents in Florida. Talking to the police, who haven't found anything yet. Talking to my aunt, Mom's sister in California. And my aunties. They're all in Maryland. They didn't even know Dad had lost his job. Mom talks and paces on the cordless. She drinks coffee and wipes down the kitchen counter over and over. She begs everyone on the phone not to come and help. She says the best thing everyone can do is think of where my father might be. That's the only thing anyone can do, she says. Everyone listens except my grandparents, who are coming anyway.

I think of my other grandparents, my Indian grandparents, who died before I was born. Dad has two black-and-white pictures of them, the only pictures I've seen. They hang in the den. They both look very serious in the pictures, even angry. I wonder how angry they'd be if they knew about this.

The next day, my grandparents arrive early in the morning carrying a big old green suitcase and a cooler filled with challah bread, frozen brisket, chicken soup, pickles, and my favorite, stuffed cabbage.

"Oh, Ma," Mom says to Grandma as she loads the food into the freezer. "You didn't have to."

Grandma waves Mom's comment away. Grandpa's already seated at the dining room table reading the paper, which is something he does a lot of.

"Max," Grandma says. "Now's not the time."

Grandpa looks at her over his bifocals. "What?" he says, but folds the paper anyway.

Grandma gives me a hard hug when she sees me. She smells the way she always smells, like a new box of tissues mixed with her flowery perfume. She brushes the hair away from my face.

"How's my girl doing?" she asks softly.

I shrug, knowing there's no way to explain. She looks at me a little longer. "Ah, the strong, silent type, like your dad," she says. Mom flashes her a look. Grandma always tells me how much I'm like my father. Normally it puffs my chest with pride, but not today. I watch my feet, twist my toe into the yellow linoleum. What an ugly kitchen floor, I think, and picture Kate's kitchen floor, shiny black and white tiles. Grandma opens her mouth, flustered, realizing her mistake. She seems about to say something else, but then Natasha comes running down the stairs.

"Grammy, Gramps!" she yells. She runs over to Grandma and leaps into her arms. While Grandma is busy fussing over her, I sit next to Grandpa.

"Can we do cartoons?" I ask him. He can draw anything. His sketches of me and Natasha hang in our bedrooms. He also teaches me how to draw my favorite comic strips out of the newspaper. Mostly I do Peanuts.

He nods and finds the right page and takes two pencils

out of his breast pocket. He always carries a few with him. They're the right kind for drawing, dark and chalky.

He draws Snoopy's nose on the edge of the paper and I copy him. He draws the rest of his head and I copy him. By the end I have a perfect Snoopy sitting on his doghouse. When I try to draw cartoons on my own, they look like little-kid drawings, all wavy and shaped funny.

"Grandpa?" I say. He looks up at me over his bifocals. His gray hair is longer on one side than the other. He combs the longer side over his bald spot, but it always falls back, giving him lopsided hair. He doesn't seem to care, though. Grandma is always smoothing the long side back over his head for him. "Where do you think Dad is?" If anyone might know it's probably Grandpa, since he's a man, and a dad, and loves me.

He leans back in his chair and taps his pencil on the paper.

"I don't know," he finally says, and sees my face fall. "I wish I did, we all do. But I'm sure there's an explanation for all this. I'm sure he's fine."

"Really?" I say. "How are you sure?"

He leans in close and kisses me on the top of my head. "I'm sure, because I wish to be. Simple as that. You want to do some more?" he asks.

"No," I say. "I'm kind of tired. I'm gonna take a nap." Suddenly I want to cry again, but not in front of Grandpa. I get up and walk past the kitchen, where Grandma and Natasha are starting a batch of cookies. I wonder where Mom is and go to look for her. Her door is closed; I press my ear to it. She's crying. Right now it seems like the only thing that makes any sense. I knock.

"Yes?" she asks.

"It's Sonia," I say. She answers the door with red eyes and a tissue in her hand. She takes my hand and we sit on the bed.

"Are you okay?" I ask.

"No, but I will be."

"I want to lie down, Mom."

"Me too," she says, and we both lie down on the bed. I curl into her and she puts her arms around me.

"Mom?" I ask with my eyes closed.

"Yes," she says.

"What if Dad never comes back?" I can't say what I really mean, but Mom must know. She must be thinking it too.

"We have to take this a day at a time," she says, smoothing my hair back. "What we know today is that there are lots of smart people out there looking for him."

"But—"

"Sonia," she interrupts. "We have to believe in your dad. He wouldn't leave us like this. He wouldn't . . ."

Her voice trails off and she hugs me tighter and all the hard stuff between us melts away.

It's dark when I wake and I see a figure standing in the

doorway. Dad, I think. He's home. It was all just a mistake, or a dream. I sit up and squint into the lighted doorway. It's not Dad. It's Grandma, and Natasha's standing beside her like a little ghost in her white nightgown.

"She wants to sleep in here," Grandma says. Mom lifts up the blankets for Natasha to get in. And she does.

For the next three nights, Natasha and I sleep in Mom's bed. Grandma cooks us big, hot meals of brisket or chicken with lots of gravy and bread, hardly a vegetable in sight. I just eat, sleep, play cards with Grandma, draw cartoons with Grandpa, and try to pretend there isn't a hole as big as the Grand Canyon in my heart.

Something about all this, though—the cuddling in bed like kittens, the warm, heavy food sitting in my stomach, my grandparents treating me special—feels good, feels like a holiday. There's a part of me that doesn't want this coziness to end. There's a part of me that doesn't want Dad to come back if he's going to be sad and empty and ruin it.

On Friday, Kate calls.

"Are you okay?" she asks when I answer the phone. Her voice sounds different, tiny.

"Yeah," I say, and wonder if somehow she's heard.

"How come you haven't been in school? Are you sick?"

"No." I let the quiet that follows hang there like a soaked towel, wet and heavy.

"What's going on?" she says finally. "Is this about Peter's party? I didn't know I made you so upset."

I have to smile. Kate thinks I'm staying home because of her.

"It has nothing to do with that. I don't even care anymore."

"Oh." She sounds disappointed.

"It's my dad. He's—" I start to say, but I can't tell her. "He's in the hospital. He has pneumonia, but he'll be okay."

"Oh, no. Well, I'm glad he's going to be okay," she says, not questioning it. "So are you going to be at the game tomorrow?"

"I can't. We have to visit him."

"Can't you go after?"

"I don't think so. The game's during visiting hours." God, how I wish it were true. I picture bringing Dad a big bouquet of flowers at the hospital. He smiles a happy, weak smile when he sees me, and the best part is that he's not going anywhere.

"Well, I guess we'll have to change the halftime routine."

"I'm sorry," I say. "Hey, Kate?"

"Yeah?"

"I have to go." I don't even bother to give her a reason before hanging up. I wish Kate were a different person. I wish I could have told her the truth and trusted her with it, but after the way she acted at the party, I see her whispering to Jess at lunch, thrilled that she has the most interesting story to tell at the table. I want so badly to talk to someone who's not Mom, Natasha, Grandma, or Grandpa. I dial before I can think about it too long.

"Hi," I say to Sam, and as soon as I hear her voice I start to cry.

"Sonia? What's wrong?"

I tell her everything. About Kate, Peter's party, Danny's kiss, watching Kate and Jess at the party, that last year feels like another universe, a much better one. I tell her I'm jealous that she gets to be there in that universe and I don't. I tell her that I miss her.

"I was jealous of you," she said. "You have your big new school, new friends, cheerleading. What do you need me for?"

"Who else am I going to have ESP with?" I say, laughing, but still sort of crying too.

Then I tell her about Dad. She listens quietly.

"The worst part is that I can't do anything. I just have to wait. It's the hardest waiting I've ever done. It makes me feel sick to my stomach."

That's when she gets an idea. She runs and gets her Magic 8 Ball and asks *the* question: Is my dad coming home?

"I'm shaking it," Sam says, fast and breathy.

I chew the hard skin around my thumb.

"Oh," she says.

"What?"

"It's just a stupid Magic Eight Ball."

"What? What did it say?" I try to swallow, but my mouth has gone as dry as paper.

"It says, *My reply is no.*"

"No?"

"*My reply is no,*" Sam says.

chapter twenty-four

That Monday, Natasha and I go back to school, Mom goes back to work, and my grandparents go back to Florida. We all go back to sleeping in our own beds. It's a short week, anyway, because of Thanksgiving. Mom says we'll wait to celebrate when Dad comes home. That's okay with me. I couldn't imagine having Thanksgiving without him either.

The police say that Dad took out a thousand dollars in cash at the airport on the day he was supposed to fly to Hong Kong. But Mom already knew that. She looked up their bank statement on the computer. So much for the police, she said after they told her. The police say it's a good sign that he took out the money. I keep hearing Sam's voice telling me about the Magic 8 Ball. *My reply is no,* it says to me all day long in my classes. I want to stick my fingers in my ears to drown it out.

People know now in school. Mom called the principal to

tell her what was going on and she told my teachers. Somehow every person in school, and maybe the town, and maybe the world, has found out. I assume this because no one has looked me in the eye this week except Alisha. She keeps trying to catch my attention in English, but I just keep staring at Mrs. Langley like she's saying the most interesting thing I've ever heard.

When the next bell rings, I try to disappear into the crowd of kids rushing off to their lockers, hoping no one says anything to me. Then I hear my name. I ignore it, not even sure where it's coming from until I feel a tap on my shoulder. Mrs. Langley is standing right behind me.

"I want to talk to you," she says. "It will only take a second."

I follow her to her classroom, wondering what I could have done. I haven't been passing notes or anything. She pulls up a chair by her desk and motions for me to sit down. I do and cross my arms tightly over my chest.

"I'm sorry about what you're going through," she says. Her voice sounds different, lower, almost gentle.

I look down at my knees. "Thanks," I mumble, not really knowing how I'm supposed to be. Should I act really sad, or pretend I'm okay, like it doesn't bother me?

"I've wanted to say this to you for a while, and maybe this isn't the right time, but I know how smart you are, Sonia. I can tell by your writing assignments, but I know I haven't seen what you can really do."

"I miss my old school," I blurt out, the tears springing to my eyes.

"I know you do, but there's always something new to learn wherever you are."

I nod.

"I understand your mind is elsewhere right now, but remember, I'm here to help. Don't be afraid to ask."

I just nod again. She stands up and hands me a tissue. I take it, give her a half smile, and rush off to my next class.

At lunch I quietly eat my avocado, Swiss cheese, and sprout sandwich at the end of Kate's table, trying to be invisible. Mrs. Langley's words play over in my head. Was she nice to me because she felt sorry for me? Has she really thought I was smart all this time, even when she gave me a D on my vocabulary test?

Jess and another Jessica whisper together at the other end of the table and take sneaky sideways glances at me. Kate sits by them, but doesn't whisper. She's leaning back in her chair eating M&M's, and glances, but not in a sneaky way, in my direction. Then she gets up and comes over.

"I heard about your dad. I'm sorry," she says. I hate the way everyone's talking about him like he's dead.

Then she leans in to give me a hug. I take it with a stiff back and arms straight at my sides.

"Thanks," I mumble into my sandwich.

She pulls away from me, her blue eyes blinking and sad for me. She looks like she's about to cry.

"What were they saying about me?" I ask.

"Who?" She reaches back and smooths her braid. I've noticed she does this in awkward moments.

"Jess and Jessica."

"Nothing," she says. "It wasn't about you."

"Yeah, right," I say. A piece of sprout is stuck between my back top teeth. I move it around with my tongue, but stuck it stays. Kate sits in a chair next to me and strokes her braid with both hands. Neither one of us says anything. I go back to eating my sandwich, wondering how I got so mean.

"Jess makes fun of people when she's nervous . . . or when she's jealous."

"Jealous of who?"

"Well, *you,* since we've been friends."

"Why do you like her if she does that?"

"She's been my friend forever. Our moms are best friends and she's really funny."

I thought I was the funny one. She goes on.

"I guess she can be kind of stupid too. But she's always been there. For me."

I just shrug.

"You know my dad isn't my real dad," Kate says. At the

word "real," my heart starts to beat faster and the stale, oily smells of everyone's chicken nuggets turn my stomach.

"He's not?" I say so quietly I can barely hear myself.

"My real dad left me and my mom six years ago. But I hardly remember him now."

My eyes blur with tears. It's hard for me to breathe. This isn't what I want to know about her.

"I know what it feels like, Sonia," she says, and puts her hand on my arm.

"My dad's coming back. He didn't leave us." I look at her and wish that I could forget everything that's happened. I wish we could be best friends in the same way Sam and I were and maybe still are. But I can't forget that Kate's not Sam. I turn away, the tears falling and falling. She lets go of my arm and walks away.

The bell rings and I get up with the crowd of kids moving toward the front doors, the doors that will take me to classes for three more hours. I hear someone calling my name. Once, and then again. I can tell it's Alisha, but I can't talk to anyone else, especially her. She's going to tell me she's sorry and then she'll probably want a sorry from me. Maybe she thinks we'll hug and make up and everything will be back to normal, like Kate did. But there is no normal for me anymore.

I walk with the crowd faster and faster down the windowed hallway, and when one of the lunch aides turns her head I slip into the bathroom. I pray Alisha doesn't follow me in. When the sound of voices dies down, and I hear the click of grown-up shoes pass the bathroom door outside, I walk out and keep walking. Then I'm running, running down the hallways, past the closed classrooms, past the lady at the front desk who calls out, "Young lady!" I push through the brown doors into the crisp fall sunshine and sprint as fast as I can off the school grounds.

I finally stop at the top of a big hill to catch my breath. I'm not sure how far it is to walk home, but if it only takes ten minutes to drive to school it can't be that far. After a few more hills, I need to rest again. I wonder how long it will take my teachers to know I'm gone. I leave the road and walk into the woods. My feet step on the fallen leaves, making a crisp, satisfying sound. *Crunch, crunch, crunch.* When my mind starts to wander—thoughts of Kate hugging me, or Alisha's face when I told her I couldn't read her book, or Sam's voice telling me what the Magic 8 Ball said—I just crunch the leaves harder. The birds in the trees add a melody. The trickle of water in a stream somewhere tickles the air.

After a lot of crunching I step out onto the road. Up ahead is an open field. Did I make a left instead of a right when I left the school? Or maybe I went straight past a road I should have turned on. I walk into the field and the soft grass collapses quietly under my feet. I decide to sit and then lie down. The ground against my back is cool and damp. The silver-white sky shimmers above, and I watch the film of clouds moving across it as my limbs grow heavier. I sink into the ground and let the flat, solid feeling fill me, fill up all those empty spaces I didn't know I had.

chapter twenty-five

Something soft touches my forehead and wakes me up. It's dark and cold, really cold. I'm shivering. A moving light flashes above me then disappears. Someone's hair brushes against my face.

"Sonia," my mother's voice calls to me. She's crying. I sit up and realize she's holding me, rocking me. I feel the waves of her weeping against me. Then she stops crying, stops holding me, puts her hands on my shoulders, and looks me hard in the eye.

She opens her mouth to say something, but doesn't. Then she gathers me in again. I look up and see another person there in the woods with me—a policeman—and he shines a flashlight in my face. I squint and turn away. I have so many questions, but it's easier not to speak. It's easier to close my eyes again.

The policeman drives fast in the dark and the car rides smoother than any car I've ever been in, like I'm gliding on air through the night. Mom and I sit in the back. I'm still shivering, even though I'm covered in Mom's coat and a blanket that the policeman gave me. I lean against Mom and she runs her fingers through my hair.

"Why?" I ask. "Why did Dad do this? Does he hate us?"

"Of course he doesn't hate us." She looks out the window. I wait for her to say something else.

"You scared me, Sonia, and I'm very angry at you for that." Her face is drawn and her mouth tight.

"I'm sorry. I really am."

"I realize you can't understand what it feels like not to know where your daughter is. To drive around in a police car searching on the sides of roads praying she's okay. It's an awful feeling, worse than not knowing where Dad is."

I swallow hard and cover my face with my hands. They smell like dirt.

"I wasn't thinking, I just wanted to . . ." I pause to think about what I really did want. I didn't want to scare Mom and make her feel worse than she already does. "I just wanted to be somewhere new," I manage.

Mom is quiet. She plays with her gold and ruby bracelet, twisting it slowly around her wrist. "I ran away once too."

"You did? When?"

"When your dad asked me to marry him," she says. "I was

scared that my parents wouldn't accept that I wanted to marry an Indian man. I needed to think apart from everyone."

"Where'd you go?"

"I went to Israel. I had always wanted to go there, and it just seemed like the right place, the place I had to go to make my decision. I finally called my mom and she wouldn't speak to me. She didn't speak to me until my wedding day six months later. And it wasn't because I was marrying your dad, although she wasn't happy about it. It was because I disappeared on her. It's a terrible thing to do to people you love, but I guess sometimes it feels like there's no other option. Some people need to be alone for a while to learn how to listen to themselves again."

I wonder if that's what I was doing, listening. "Are you going to not speak to me for six months?" I ask.

"I'm speaking to you now, aren't I?" She grips my hand. "I may have to go away for a while myself. I can't just sit and wait around for the police anymore. I've got to try and find him. Grandma and Grandpa will come stay again. Will you be okay with that? I wanted to tell you before"—she sweeps her hand across the backseat of the police car—"all this happened."

I nod.

She turns and stares hard at me. "I need you to promise me, Sonia, that you won't do anything like this again. If you can't, you need to tell me and I won't go. But I can't ever go through this again."

"I promise," I say.

"You're sure?"

As I let her words sink in, I feel strangely relaxed. If anyone can find Dad, Mom can. "I'm sure," I say, and sink back into the leather seat. Finally, I stop shivering.

chapter twenty-six

I've drawn eleven different Snoopys in the last hour. One's reading a book, another is flying a kite. Another one is driving a car. Another one's diving into a pool. I even made one doing a cartwheel. Grandpa looks each one over and either shows me how to make one look more three-dimensional or nods in approval.

Grandma's busy making Shabbat dinner. It's Friday. Mom's been gone for two days. First she spent a day asking around in local places. A man at a gas station said he might have seen Dad, but that was two weeks ago, so it isn't much help. She asked at a bunch of motels in the area, but no one else had seen him. Now she's in Maryland, where my aunties live. The police said she should look in all the places that Dad's been to, that most people who run away go to a place they've been before.

Grandma's unwrapping paper plates, cups, even paper bowls, and stirring soup in the special pot that Mom keeps separate from our regular pots. We have to eat on paper since our regular plates aren't kosher and Grandma and Grandpa are.

"Grandma," I say, getting up from my drawing, following the smell of chicken soup, "why are you kosher?"

Grandma stops stirring and looks at me. "Because my parents were and my grandparents were and my great-grandparents were."

"But Mom doesn't do what you do." I look in the pot and take a sniff. The smooth, warm smell of the chicken and egg noodles calms me. Then I face Grandma again. I wonder if Mom told her about what I said to Jackie?

Grandma smiles. "Well, your mother decided to create new traditions. But it's important for me to keep my parents' traditions. It makes me feel connected to them even though they're not living anymore. I've come to understand, though, that people stay connected in different ways. And I've even changed some of my ways—like cooking in your nonkosher kitchen."

"Were you mad at Mom for marrying Dad?"

Grandma clears her throat. "I was," she says, going back to her soup. "See, you have to understand how important it is to keep Judaism alive. There aren't many of us. If we don't respect the traditions that have given guidance and knowledge and comfort to so many people, we could disappear."

The word "disappear" gives me a sudden headache. Grandma continues stirring and talking.

"I would hate to see that happen. But that was before I knew your dad. He's a wonderful man and I love him as if he were my son." Her voice cracks a little on the word "son," and she keeps her eyes down toward the steamy pot of soup. She clears her throat again.

"So you were mad just because he wasn't Jewish?" I ask.

"Yes, but I was wrong. I should have tried to understand what your mother wanted."

"What if I decide not to be Jewish? I'm barely Jewish as it is." What I don't say is that as much as I want to, I just don't feel Jewish. My name isn't Jewish. I don't look like Mom or Grandma. If I went to a Jewish school where all the kids were Jewish, they'd probably wonder what I was doing there.

"Sweetheart." Grandma puts her hands on my shoulders. "You were born to a Jewish mother, and that makes you completely Jewish, not barely. You were born a girl too, but I guess you could have a sex change if you wanted to."

"Grandma!"

"What I'm trying to tell you is that you are Jewish, even if you don't go to temple. Even if there are other parts of you. What you do with it is up to you."

"But what if I wanted to be another religion? What if I married an Indian man too and I wanted to be Hindu? Would you still love me?"

"That's another thing you were born with: my love," she says, and holds my hands tight. "There's nothing you can do to change that one."

I smile and hold on to her feathery, bony hands, her skin so light and soft it's almost translucent. My hands look really dark against hers. I stare at them, amazed that we're even related. I wonder if she ever thinks that, or if Mom ever did, holding the hands of her Indian-looking children. Did anyone ever wonder if we really belonged to her?

chapter twenty-seven

Mom's been gone for five days now; she'll be in Maryland for one more day. Tomorrow she's going to search in Massachusetts, where we go skiing every winter. I'm back in school. Mom said I could stay home, but I want to do something else besides sit there with Grandma and Grandpa, and I'll have way too much homework to catch up on. Natasha's been at school the whole time. When she's busy she seems to forget all about our weird, broken life. But that's Natasha. And even though I can't forget, I can try to pay attention to other things, like my schoolwork, for once.

At lunch I watch Kate eating the same chicken nuggets she always eats and this is what I think—she's afraid to eat anything else. I look down at my cucumber, havarti, and tomato sandwich and take another delicious bite. It makes me feel sorry for Kate.

I get up and walk over to Alisha's table. She's talking to a girl I don't really know. I sit down next to her and they stop talking and look at me. I smile the brightest smile I can muster, my heart beating hard in my ears.

Alisha just looks at me.

"Can I talk to you?" I say.

"I guess so," she says. The other girl shrugs.

"I'm sorry," I say.

"For what?" Alisha says, looking me hard in the eye. The thing with Alisha is that she can see a lie coming from miles away.

"For being a jerk about your book. For not coming over. I really want to do both those things. I want to be friends again."

Just like that, Alisha smiles. I take a deep breath and relax my shoulders, which I didn't realize were practically in my ears.

"I'm sorry too, that I haven't said anything to you since . . . since your dad." Then she doesn't say any more.

"It's okay." I swallow. "Can I sit with you?"

"Yeah," says Alisha.

I walk over to Kate's table and start gathering up my stuff. I don't look at anyone.

"What a freak," I hear Jess say to Kate as I'm leaving.

That afternoon I walk over to the field for cheering practice. It's the first practice I've been to since Dad disappeared.

Nobody looks at me, but I manage to give Jess a couple of angry stares, just so she knows I heard her in the cafeteria. She looks down at her nails, up at the sky, anywhere but at me. Kate starts some stretches, so I follow, relieved to have something to do besides stand there. As I touch my toes, I hear my name and see Alisha running up to me with her book.

"Do you want to take it now or tomorrow morning?" she says, breathless.

"No, I can take it now," I say, and stand up. I get my backpack.

Jess comes over, hands on her hips.

"What's that?" she asks as I take Alisha's notebook. "Some kind of secret diary?"

"No," Alisha says. "It's my book."

"Oh, yeah? Let me see," Jess says, and grabs the notebook out of my hands.

"Hey!" I yell, and try to grab it back. Jess holds it over her head. Alisha glares at her. I grab at it again, get my hand on it, but Jess pulls hard.

"Stop, you're going to rip it!" Alisha yells. I let go.

"God, everyone chill. I just want to read some of it," Jess says, and opens it to the middle.

"'*Marie sat on the ship not knowing what to do. She knew Jack had escaped from prison. She knew he might be dangerous. But how could that be? She loved him. He must be good, he must be,'"* Jess reads in an overly dramatic voice. "Oh, no, what are they going to do?" she says, sounding like she's all worried.

I look over at Kate. She just keeps stretching, pretending not to notice what's happening. I move as quick as lightning and whisk the notebook out of Jess's hand.

"Why are you so mean, Jess? What did Alisha ever do to you?" I say, and hand Alisha her book.

Jess just shrugs. "She walks around thinking she's better than all of us, clutching that stupid book all the time. I wanted to see what was so great about it."

"You know what?" I take a deep breath. "I don't want to be on this team anymore, especially not with you." I turn to Alisha. "Let's go," I tell her. Alisha's mouth hangs open as she looks back between Jess, Kate, and me. I pull her arm and we leave together.

"You weirdos belong to each other," Jess yells after us, then Kate calls my name and tells me to wait. I don't turn around. I just keep moving toward the buses, Alisha and I leaning against each other.

chapter twenty-eight

It's been six days since Mom left, and I'm sitting on the stairs after school taking off my shoes, which are wet from the rain. Mom would kill me for even coming into the house with them. I hear Grandma talking on the phone. She sounds so serious, it makes me listen harder. I walk over to her. She's nodding, her eyes wet, saying "okay" over and over. My body feels all tingly like the way it did when Kate told me about her dad never coming back. It's happened, the terrible thing that no one wants to talk about. Dad is never coming home. I feel dizzy and sit back down on the stairs. It seems like I'm floating above my house, above myself. I put my head in my hands to keep me down on the earth. Then Grandma's there, touching my shoulder.

"Sonia," she says. "They found your dad."

"Is he dead?" I whisper into my hands.

"Oh, sweetheart, no! No, not at all. He's going to be okay. It's all going to be okay."

Now she's crying and I'm crying. Then she gathers me to her and we sit on the stairs for a few minutes. And while Grandma holds me and we cry, I thank God. I've never really talked to God or prayed before, but now that's what I do. I'm not even sure if it's a Jewish God, or a Hindu God, or a Christian God, but it doesn't matter. I'm just thanking the one that saved Dad.

Dad had been staying in a motel near the inn on Cape Cod. He finally used his ATM card to get more cash and the detectives found him. They took him to a hospital for people dealing with problems like depression. He'll be there until he heals. We can't see him before then. I wonder if depression works like that, like a broken leg. When he heals, will he be fixed forever? Did he not heal the first time he got depressed?

When Mom gets home that night, she says the reason Dad left was that he felt too bad to be around us. He didn't want us to see him like that anymore, so he thought he was doing a good thing, and she says we shouldn't be mad at him. And I'm not, except I keep having to tell myself I'm not so that I won't be. I know I'm supposed to feel lucky, but I can't help feeling sad and mad.

✦ ✦ ✦

The next morning at school there's a pink-and-green-striped bag tied to my locker with a pink ribbon. I wonder if someone left me a gift because Dad's not missing anymore. Mom called the principal this morning before school and told her we'd found Dad, but I didn't think everyone would know by now. I untie the bag and look inside. It's the picture of me and Kate sleeping that Greg took of us. With it is a note on purple stationery in Kate's neat, fat writing.

> I know you're going through a really hard time and I feel so bad about what's happened between us. I've talked to Jess, and she's going to be better. I know she's been awful, but I still want to be friends and the team isn't the same without you. Please talk to me at lunch or call me. Please, please, please!
>
> XXXOOO
>
> Kate

My heart sinks as I read the letter. It would almost be easier if Kate would be like Jess, mean. I don't look at her in the morning and I don't go near her at lunch. I just sit with Alisha and hope Kate's not staring at me.

While I'm unwrapping a piece of Indian candy, a girl at

the table asks me if I'm black. I open my mouth and close it, not knowing what to say.

"What does it matter?" Alisha says back at her suddenly. "Why does everyone here care so much about who's who and what's what? I just don't get it," she says, waving her hands. I feel a ripple of excitement run through me. It's been a while since I felt someone was truly in my corner.

The girl shrinks in her chair. I'm starting to understand that I'm going to need to answer these questions for other people, maybe before I completely know the answers myself. The more I do, the more people will understand and the less they'll have to ask me.

"It's okay, Alisha," I say. And this is what I tell the girl: "I'm half Indian and I'm Jewish. Oh, and I'm part Polish because my grandfather's from Poland. And my grandmother's mother was from Russia, so I guess I'm part Russian too."

"Cool," the girl says, and goes back to eating her lunch.

That night I pace around the phone in the den. I pick it up. I put it down. I pick it up again and hold it to my ear, listening to the dial tone turn into a busy signal. I put it down again. I pick it up one last time and dial Kate's number. Jackie says hello, and I hang up. So stupid. They have caller ID.

Of course we don't, but a few seconds later when the phone rings I'm pretty sure I know who it is, so I just let it ring until I hear Mom pick up downstairs. I run to the top of the stairs and listen.

"Oh, I don't know. Maybe Sonia was calling. Hold on."

I hear Mom coming toward the stairs, so I dash into my room and land at my desk. I grab my math textbook and open it as if I'm just hanging out reading about math.

"Sonia, did you just call Kate?" Mom asks, standing in my doorway.

"Uh, no."

"Well, she said her mom just saw our number and then got disconnected." Mom cocks her head to the side. "You sure?"

"Yeah," I say, and make a little snorty laugh.

"Well, here's Kate," she says, handing me the cordless.

I take it and clear my throat. Mom's still standing there. I wave at her and she finally leaves.

"Hi," I say way too cheerfully.

"Did you just call me?" Kate says.

"No."

"Well, my mom said she saw your number. Are you lying?" she asks.

"No." There's silence. "Kate, are you still there?" I say after a few seconds that feel like hours.

"I'm really happy to hear that your dad's back. You're lucky."

Suddenly confessing seems a lot easier than talking

about my dad, who's supposed to be back and yet is not here at all. "Okay, I am lying."

"I knew it! Why?"

"Because, I just . . . I don't know."

"Whatever. I don't care, just please come back to the team."

Now I remember what I want to say to Kate, what I've wanted to say to her all along. "I don't understand why you want me on the team," I start. "I don't even know why you like me. And how can you like Jess and me at the same time? She's so . . ." I want to say awful, scared, idiotic, but I stop myself.

"I told you she's just jealous."

"But Kate, you still haven't answered me. Why do you want to be friends with me?"

More silence. I wait. "Because we have so much fun together," Kate says in a tiny voice. "You're just likable."

I smile.

She keeps going. "You could be so cool, you know."

I feel hot. Suddenly my cheeks are on fire. "What do you mean? Like as cool as you?"

"I didn't mean it that way, I—"

"Kate, I don't want to be like you," I tell her. I might not know exactly who I want to be, but it's definitely *not* Kate.

"I just meant—"

"I don't care what you meant. And I don't want to be on the team anymore."

"Please, Sonia, I'm really sorry."

"Me too," I say, and hang up.

I feel sort of light-headed and giggly. "Happy," I think is the word. Happy that Kate finally answered the question I've had about her all along.

chapter twenty-nine

My feet don't feel the ground as I walk up the brick lane toward a large stone building with a black front door. My hands sweat and I have to keep wiping them on my new purple corduroy skirt. When I enter the lobby what first grabs my attention is a big vase bursting with fresh flowers in every size and color. It sits on a round wooden table and is so big and beautiful that it almost seems to give off a sound—a hum. Mom holds my hand and Natasha's as we continue down the shiny marble hallway to see Dad.

Last night on the phone I told Sam I was afraid I wouldn't be able to speak, that my dad seemed like a different person now, that I didn't really know him anymore. Sam said I'd know what to say when I saw him, that just seeing his face would help. Sam always has a good answer for everything.

Dad has been sending me and Natasha postcards every

day since he's been here. He always writes that he loves and misses us. He also tells us little things about the place where he's staying. That he has a nice doctor named Roger who's helping him. That he doesn't like the food. That they have a beautiful rose garden he likes to sit in that reminds him of the rose garden his parents had in India. It's the first peaceful memory he's ever told me about India.

I've only written him back once. I taped a picture of the Taj Mahal to a card and wrote,

Thought you might like this.

Love,
Sonia

That's all I could think of saying.

Natasha writes him letters about school and her friends and the songs she's learned since he's been gone. She also decided to paint a picture of roses for him. She painted them like Chagall, all swirling reds, greens, and blues.

Mom said the reason Natasha and I weren't able to talk to him the last three weeks was that he had to concentrate on getting well. I guess I believe that, but a part of me doesn't. A part of me has no idea what to believe anymore.

Mom signs in at a desk and then we go sit on a leather couch in the lobby to wait. Natasha starts climbing all over it and tries to touch the big woven basket thing hanging on the wall, and Mom has to pull on the skirt of her dress to get her down. I've never seen Natasha so hyper. She's been that way for days, since Mom told us about visiting day. Mom says it's because she's too little to know how to talk about all her feelings, so she has to act them out.

A man with the reddest hair I've ever seen comes down the hallway. It hangs down past his ears and he pushes a wavy piece out of his eyes. When Mom sees him she pops up from the couch like something bit her and grabs my hand.

"Good to see you again," he says to Mom, and gives her a hug.

"You too, Roger," she says. She looks like she's going to cry. Then we all follow Roger toward an elevator.

When I go into Dad's room, I'm surprised to see he's wearing jeans and an old T-shirt. I hadn't expected him to be wearing a suit, but that's how I always picture him, just off the train from work. He looks so relaxed, sitting on the end of his bed, like he just got up from a really good nap.

"Daddy!" Natasha yells as soon as Mom opens the door, and crawls right into his lap. My heart speeds up as I see his arms circle her and hold her tight. He closes his eyes and presses his face into her hair. When he opens them they glisten, and it shocks me—his tears send me walking backward. I stand straight against the cool, hard wall.

"Hi, Sonia," Dad says. The words in my brain pile up into a big mess. Mom looks at me, puts out her hand for me, but

I stay against the wall. Natasha keeps cuddling in Dad's lap, telling him about her friends at school, her latest art project, what she had for dinner last night, blah, blah, blah. Mom sits in a chair and watches.

After several minutes Dad says to Mom, "How about now?"

She looks at me. "As good a time as any." She tries to hoist Natasha out of Dad's lap but Natasha hangs on for dear life, knocking off his glasses, messing up his hair.

"You'll see him in a few minutes," Mom says, and Natasha's wails drown out the rest of Mom's words. Dad kneels down, puts his hands on Natasha's arms, and talks to her so softly I can't hear him. Natasha stops crying, turns toward Mom, and buries her face in her tweedy skirt. Mom leads her out of the room.

"I wanted some time alone with you," he tells me.

I nod and swallow, trying to stop myself from running out the door after Mom and Natasha.

"I know this is hard. Roger's going to set up a time where we all meet and talk more about what's happened. He'll help us sort it out. We don't have to do it all now. I'm coming home next week."

I wiggle my toes and rock back and forth, ball to heel.

"You must be angry with me," he says.

I nod again.

"You must wonder what kind of person I am," he says. "If I'm still the same father."

More nodding.

"I'll always be your dad," he says. "I'll always love you like I do."

"How?" I say under my breath, and wonder if the thought in my head actually made it through my mouth and out into the room.

"How what?" he asks as he smooths the front of his hair.

"How do you love me?"

He takes off his glasses and wipes them on his shirt. Then he holds them up to the light and puts them on again. "Do you know that I chose your name?" he asks.

"I thought Mom found it in an Indian children's book."

"She found the book and asked me to read it. When I read it I told her that if we had a daughter, I wanted to name her after Sonia in the book. It was the most special name I could think of."

I nod again and my eyes scan the room. It looks like a hotel room, with a little table and chair in the corner, a big bed in the middle, and a dresser to the side. A picture of sunflowers in a vase hangs on the wall. Next to the bed, I see Dad's old pair of brown leather slippers. He's had them as long as I can remember and I've tried them on many times, always amazed at how big his feet are.

"Listen to me," he says, and I look up. He sounds stern, but his eyes are soft. "In the story, Princess Sonia can do all these magical things. She can fly. She can spin gold. She's the smartest, kindest, most beautiful girl anybody has ever known, and to me she doesn't even compare to you."

"Is that what you really think?" I ask.

"I thought it on the day you were born and I only think it more every day."

"You should have told me that before," I say, and walk over to the side of the bed where the slippers are.

"You're right. I should have."

And then without thinking about it, I walk over to the slippers. I take off my uncomfortable black loafers and put the slippers on. I sit down on the bed and swing my feet back and forth. The slippers are still warm inside and feel exactly the way I remember them.

"Why don't you ever want to go back to India?"

He thinks for a minute. "Did I say that?"

"Yes."

"I didn't mean it." He thinks some more. "I went through some sad things there. We lived through the partition. We had to leave our home. My parents died there. But I don't mean to make it a sad place for you. India will always be where I became the person I am, and a part of who you are too. It's funny. I've lived in this country for twenty years, and people still look at me as a foreigner. I don't even have an accent anymore. Sometimes it can be, well, tiring, to always feel different." He takes a deep breath like he's tired just saying it.

"Yes, I know."

"You do know, don't you," he says, and squeezes my arm.

"Sometimes it feels like I'm the only one like me."

"We all feel like that for one reason or another. But I'll tell you one thing."

"What's that?"

"There is only one Sonia. And the rarer the thing, the more special it is."

"Like the Taj Mahal."

"Exactly," he says.

I think of the Taj and its mind-boggling wholeness. I think about all the parts needed to make it the way it is, the slabs of marble and stone, the thousands of jewels, the mortar, the dirt underneath. The image spins around and around in my head, all those pieces coming together to make one thing—one beautiful whole thing.

Dad sits next to me and we both stay quiet for a while until Mom, Natasha, and Roger come back in. Roger talks about the meetings we'll have once a week as a family once Dad comes home. Dad says his company is giving him a few months off, and after that, he'll see if he's ready to go back. He'll continue to see Roger once a week by himself. I ask him if he's ever going to leave us again. He says he might have times when he feels sad during his life, but he understands himself a lot more now. If he ever feels that low again, he'll spend some time at the hospital instead of leaving. It's scary to think he could feel that way again. But there are no hard secrets anymore. Nothing is too scary to talk about, Mom says to me and Natasha.

After a while I'm not really listening, though. I'm just thinking about the slippers on my feet and how, when I leave here today, I'm going to ask Dad if I can take them with me.

And how I know he'll let me without even asking why.

Then we go home, Mom, Natasha, and I. It's hard to say goodbye to Dad, but I wear the slippers in the car and I wear them to bed. That night I dream about being a princess. I can fly in this dream. I fly over Dad at the hospital and he sees me and waves. I fly over school and see Alisha and Kate. I fly back home. Except home isn't my house. It's the Taj Mahal, and my entire family is waiting for me. Mom, Natasha, and Dad. They're having a picnic. I come and sit down and suddenly we're all back home, at my real home. When I wake up this is what I think: We need to go somewhere, my family and I, when Dad gets home, somewhere really nice like the ocean. We'll have a picnic. It won't matter if it's cold. We'll just bundle up and stay close. If we do that, I think we'll be okay.

acknowledgments

It takes a village to raise a child *and* to publish a book. I would like to send out my grateful appreciation to the village that helped make this book possible. To my very wise editor, Françoise Bui, who believed in Sonia's voice and helped me give her an even bigger one, and to everyone at Delacorte Press who supported this book. To my agent, the ever-encouraging Sara Crowe, who plucked me out of the pile and put me on the map. To my friends Alexandra Cooper and Gwendolyn Gross, for their early reads and great editorial advice. To my supportive family, who always believed in me—my parents, Anita and Hiro Hiranandani; my sister, Shana Hiranandani; my sister in-law, Netania Shapiro; my in-laws, Phyllis and Hank Beinstein; my sister- and brother-in-law, Debra and David Stein; my niece, Sophie Stein; and my nephews, Zev and Leo Hiranandani and Fred and Julius Stein. Most of all, I'd like to thank my children, Hannah and Eli, and my best reader and best friend, my husband, David Beinstein. I couldn't have done this without you.

about the author

Veera Hiranandani started writing stories pretty much as soon as she started reading them. She received her MFA in fiction writing from Sarah Lawrence College and has written fiction for children and adults. Besides being a writer, she is also a Montessori teacher. Veera lives in New York with her husband, daughter, and son. This is her first novel for young readers. Visit her website at veerahiranandani.com.